Caper Finds a Clue

A Tiny House Mystery, Book Three

By Cynthia Hickey

Published by: Winged Publications

ISBN-13: 978-1-947523-59-3

DEDICATION

To All Those who eagerly await the next book

Chapter One

"Nothing makes a person need a vacation more than a kidnapping," Mags said between bites of her bacon and egg burrito. She picked up a napkin from the picnic table and dabbed at her lips. "After the jewel heist fiasco, we could use a vacation. Especially you, CJ Turley."

"What were you thinking we could do?" I could use a couple of days off.

"Float the river."

Eric Drake, local park ranger, who also happened to be my boyfriend, spewed coffee. "Sorry. Do either of you know anything about the river?"

Mags grinned. "No, that's why you're invited, too. We can rent a canoe for the day. People sometimes use kayaks, but I'm not coordinated enough. Now that I'm out of that cursed boot from my foot surgery, I need some fun."

"You didn't think finding the jewel thief was fun?" I asked, wiggling my eyebrows.

"I most certainly did," she said. "But we can't always depend on a theft or a murder to liven things up. We need to act like normal people sometimes. Call this a day away from it all." She grinned.

"One day doesn't a vacation make anyway," I said.

Eric exhaled heavily. "I know you well enough to know you won't quit until you get your way. How about we go today? I've nothing pressing on my schedule, and it's always a good idea to scout out who's on the river."

"I don't have anything going on either." I stood and gathered up our trash. "We can have a picnic somewhere along the way." The more I thought of spending the day on the water, the more excited I became. I could use a day off. Even better, I'd spend the day with Eric…and Mags, but since I rarely was without my middle-aged friend, I went along with it for the most part.

Inside my tiny house, I opened one of the drawers under the stairs and pulled out a sheet of copy paper. I scribbled that I'd be back later that evening and to contact Roy Owens, our all-around handyman, if there was an emergency. After tacking the paper to my front door, I sent Roy a text informing him I'd be gone for the day. Next I packed three sandwiches, several water bottles, some dog snacks, and a bag of chips, then clipped Caper's leash to her collar and joined Eric and Mags outside.

Mags eyed my dog. "I suppose we do have to take her."

"Why wouldn't we?" I narrowed my eyes.

"She tends to find trouble."

True. "Not this time." *Please, Lord, not this*

time. It seemed my dog had a talent for finding stolen jewelry, which resulted in trouble, which proved Mags's point.

We piled into Eric's side-by-side, which to me seemed like a cross between a golf cart and a jeep. "Not you, CJ. You need to follow me. Someone will have to give us a ride back to the truck. Mags will stay with the canoe."

"Right." I hadn't thought of that. "Good thinking."

I followed in my car to his place, where he slid a canoe onto a trailer, hitched the trailer to a real jeep, and waited for Mags to climb in. Half an hour later, Eric had me park at the exit point, then join him and Mags. How complicated a simple canoe trip could be.

"Life jackets." He tossed us each one. "No exceptions."

"We're going to sweat all the way to our toes," Mags grumbled, sliding into hers. "I hate sweat."

"Remember, it was your idea to go canoeing in the summer." Eric grinned.

"Here's hoping for a breeze," I said, climbing into the canoe with Caper. I set my dog on the middle seat where Mags would sit and took my place in the front. It would be up to Eric and me to do the paddling.

We floated past cliffs and trees, waterfalls and meadows. The river truly was one of God's greatest creations. I set the canoe paddle on my lap, and the tension of the last month left my shoulders. Tension from being responsible for not only the tiny house community, but the neighboring campground when its overseer had taken a vacation. There was also the theft and the manslaughter that kept me busy between the two, not to mention someone had tried to hurt my dog. I clenched my fists at the thought, then took a deep breath to relax. "It's beautiful," I said, glancing over my shoulder at Eric.

"One of my favorite places." He gave a lopsided smile. "Maybe you and I can come here sometime without the third wheel."

"I heard that." Mags crossed her arms. "If you didn't want me along, all you had to do was say so."

"It was your idea," he laughed. "We couldn't ditch you."

A couple of men floated past on kayaks, heads low over their paddles. Soon after, more kayaks floated by carrying both men and women.

"Quite the gathering," I said.

"Most likely a club. There are several in the area." Eric renewed his paddling. "This river can become crowded at times. Then other times, it's as if I'm the only person left on the planet."

"You do this a lot?" I asked.

"Every chance I get."

I needed to start going with him. During the years of caring for my dying grandmother, I'd had little fun. I didn't begrudge those years but counted them a blessing as I got to spend my grandmother's last days with her. But now, I had to make up for lost time. Eric was my first real boyfriend, and it took me a while to learn how not to look like an idiot around him. I also had treasured friends of whom Mags was one, and although I'd inherited Grams's house, I loved the simplicity of my tiny house and my job as overseer of the community. Someday, I'd have to clean out Grams's house and decide whether to live there or sell. Today was not that day.

"Here's a good spot to have lunch." Eric steered us to a low edge of the bank cleared of trees. "It looks as if several others have been here before us." He pointed to scrapes in the dirt.

"Well, they're gone now," Mags announced, squeezing past me. "I need to plant my feet on firm ground for a bit and eat something."

"I second that." My legs protested at first but stretched out soon enough. I helped Eric pull the canoe far enough on the bank so it wouldn't float off, then grabbed the backpack I'd put our lunches in.

We each found a log or a boulder to sit on and dug into our lunches while Caper nosed around the area. "Stay, Caper."

She wagged her tail without looking at me and kept on about her business.

"She won't go far," Eric said.

"That's what you think. That dog is a wanderer." I bit into my turkey-and-Swiss sandwich, keeping an eye on my ill-trained, furry friend.

"Relax, sweetheart." Eric gave me a wink. "There isn't much trouble she can get into out here unless she rustles up a snake or a skunk."

"If there's trouble, she'll find it. Why do you think Grams named her Caper?" I raised my eyebrows.

With a laugh, he opened the bag of potato

chips. "I've always wanted a dog, but a big one. I doubt a Labrador would fit in my house."

"Black or chocolate?" Mags asked.

"Are we talking candy?" I hoped so. I hadn't thought to pack anything sweet.

"Colors of labs." She rolled her eyes. "Of course, you can also get yellow."

"Chocolate," Eric said. "I would name her Hershey."

"Cute." I made a mental note to find a way to get him a chocolate-colored lab. He spent enough time outside that the dog would get plenty of exercise. Eric had helped me enough times to warrant me doing something nice for him. Oh, no. Caper was nowhere in sight. "Where is that darn dog?"

"We'll get her before we leave. Don't worry." Eric guzzled a bottle of water. "Humid today." He removed his life jacket, then his shirt.

Mags's eyes widened, then she glanced at me with a grin and fanned herself.

My face heated. I'd seen photos of well-developed men without a shirt, but Eric could grace every month of my calendar. He stood and ambled into the water.

"You might want to cool off, too," Mags said. "Your face is red."

"Hush." I did remove my lifejacket so the breeze could cool my sweat.

"That felt great." Eric shook his head, spraying us with water, then donned his shirt.

"Not necessary to give us a shower, young man." Mags wiped water from her face. "We should get going so we're home by supper."

We just ate and already she's thinking about food. I pushed to my feet and called for my dog. "Caper! Come here, girl."

Eric gave a shrill whistle.

Caper came running and dropped something at my feet.

"Is that a finger?" Mags squinted.

Chapter Two

"No. It's a, uh—" Definitely a finger, but I didn't want to admit that my dog had done it again—he'd found something best left alone. At least it wasn't diamonds or jewelry. I tried without success to find a bright side.

"That is definitely a finger," Eric said. He pulled a napkin from my backpack and wrapped it around the appendage. "The body this belongs to must be here somewhere."

"Here we go again," I mumbled.

"Just because Caper found a body part doesn't mean there's a mystery for you to get involved in." Eric shook his head. "If there is a body, then this is police business."

"I have no intention of getting involved."

Mags laughed. "I've heard that before."

I shrugged. I'd said those very words at least twice before and always let myself be drawn into dangerous situations. "Lead on." I waved a hand for

Eric to take the front.

He headed in the direction from which Caper had run. “Spread out. Watch for snakes.”

About fifty yards in, I stumbled over the legs of a man and plunged headfirst into a sticker bush. “Found him.” He was missing all of his fingers and his teeth. Whoever had killed him must have dropped the index finger. Someone obviously didn’t want the identity of the victim known.

“Do you think he’s one of the kayakers who passed us?” Mags asked.

“Could be.” Eric squatted next to the body and patted his pockets. “No identification. CJ, call Davis.”

I pulled my cell phone from my pack. No service. I held it as high as I could. “I got nothing.”

Eric groaned. “We’ll have to mark where we found him and hope he’s still here when the cops come.”

“Take off your shirt again and tie it around a tree,” Mags suggested.

“I have a bandanna,” I offered, tossing her a stern look. Was she nuts? I couldn’t focus with a shirtless Eric. “How much further do we have to go?”

“We’re halfway.” Eric marched back to where we’d stopped and held the canoe steady while we climbed in. “We’ll have to speed up the pace. I don’t have to tell you what this humidity will do to a body.”

“I don’t have to tell you that I’m not returning with you later.” I shuddered.

As we paddled, questions went through my

mind like white water roaring over boulders. Who was the victim? Why was he important enough that someone wanted his identity kept a secret? Where did they dispose of the fingers and teeth?

"Stop it," Eric said. "I see the steam coming from your ears. You've already sunk your teeth into this."

I glanced over my shoulder. "No, I haven't. I have no connection with that man whatsoever, so no reason to get involved. I'm only passing the time."

"Uh huh."

I huffed and faced the river again. Last time, I couldn't help but get involved because Caper kept bringing me diamonds. The time before that, someone had hidden stolen items under my tiny house. This time was different. There was no reason to go any further just because my dog found a severed finger.

By the time we arrived at the exit point on the river, we were hot, sweaty and grumpy. Mags agreed to remain with the canoe while Eric and I went to fetch the other vehicle.

"She'll be safe, right?" I asked, watching Mags grow smaller in my rearview mirror.

"Of course." He cut me a sideways glance. "You haven't made any killers mad at you yet."

I laughed. "I'll do my best not to." While I drove, Eric placed a call to Davis.

"He said he'll meet us at your house and to call him when we arrive."

"I guess that means you'll be returning here today."

"We have to get back to the body before the

sun goes down." He rested his hand on my knee. "It isn't the first supper we've missed together because of my job."

"I know, but I look forward to alone time with you." I parked next to his jeep.

He leaned over and gave me a lingering kiss. "I'll make it up to you." He shoved the door open and jogged to his car.

~

Davis met us at my house a little after five. He took one look at me and Mags and shook his head. "Can't you two stay out of trouble?"

"It was a simple canoe ride." I crossed my arms. "Don't you have a job to do?"

"Yes, and I don't want you interfering." He motioned for Eric to get in his truck and they drove away.

"When is the new tenant for number ten arriving?" Mags poured more tea into the glass in front of me.

"His things were supposed to be delivered last night. I left the key under the mat so he could move in without waiting for morning." I glanced toward the dark house. "Doesn't look as if he's there."

"That house has a revolving door."

I agreed. First a murderer, then a strange married couple who made personalized fragrances, now a man I had yet to lay eyes on. "Maybe the house is cursed."

"Do you really believe in that stuff?" She raised her eyebrows.

"No." I sipped my tea and watched the setting sun kiss the lake. It had become my favorite way of unwinding after a long day. I preferred Eric at my side but still gazed over the water each evening whether I sat alone or not.

Caper leaned against my leg. I scratched her ears. What was I going to do with a dog that kept bringing me…things?

"They won't be back until late," Mags pointed out. "At least ten. Maybe later."

"I'll wait."

Ten p.m. came with no sign of Eric or Davis, and tiredness won out over waiting. I snapped my fingers for Caper to follow me into the house and went to bed.

The sound of a key turning in the lock of my door woke me at daybreak. I sat up and peered down into the main living space to see a tired-looking Eric plop onto my sofa. "I'll be right down and make coffee."

"That sounds wonderful."

I threw on my clothes and thundered down the stairs to the Keurig. One minute later, I set a cup of coffee on the table in front of the sofa. "Bad night?" Stupid. Moving a dead body wouldn't make for a good one.

"The body wasn't there. We finally found it in a shallow grave deeper in the woods. Someone definitely didn't want it found."

"No idea who it is?"

"Not unless we find a picture of him with his name." He turned his head. "Sorry to wake you, but I knew you'd want to know. And once I get to my bed, I won't be up for a while."

"I understand. Thanks for easing my curiosity."

"Anytime." He smiled. "Give me a kiss, then I'm off to bed."

I was more than happy to oblige, and after he left, I curled up on the sofa and fell asleep. Caper woke me at eight, whining to go out. "Okay, girl." I slipped my feet into flip-flops and stepped onto my miniature porch. While my dog did her business, I leaned over the railing and glanced at house number ten. Still no car.

Hmm. I headed in that direction, leaving Caper to follow. On the porch, I lifted the doormat to find the key still in place. Cupping my hands around my eyes, I peered into the house. Empty. Not a single box.

I pulled my cell phone from my pocket and flipped through the renter contact numbers until I found his, then pressed call and waited. When the automatic reply told me to leave a message, I did. "Yes, Mr. Smith, this is CJ Turley, the overseer at Heavenly Acres. Do you have a move-in date? Please call me at this number. Thank you."

Nothing more I could do until the man either called or showed up. I'd give him three days, then send a refund check for his deposit to the address I had on file.

"Hey, CJ." Rose waved from the swing set in the common area. The girl had been a big help when Mags needed surgery on her foot. Now, she looked as if the boredom of summer had settled in.

"Hey, yourself."

"Mags said y'all found a dead body along the river."

"Mags has a big mouth." If you wanted news

spread, all you had to do was tell Mags.

"Do the new people have any kids?" She motioned her head toward number ten.

"Nope. Just a single man in his thirties." I chuckled at the disappointed expression on her face. The only other teenager, Danny Olson, spent his summer days mowing around the lake. I'd try and come up with a summer job for Rose.

"Good morning." Mags waved from her flower bed. "You slept in."

"Eric came by at dawn." I told her what he and Davis had found.

"Somebody really doesn't want that man found," she said. "The question is why." She glanced toward house number ten. "A mystery to go right along with where your newest tenant is." She turned to me with wide eyes.

"You think they might be one and the same?" My heart stilled. "That's a stretch, Mags."

"But, what if? Have you tried googling the guy? Did his references check out?"

I nodded. "Of course, his references are good. I don't rent to them otherwise."

"Falsified." She wiggled her finger at me. "Mark my words. Something is wonky in Heavenly Acres."

"Fine. I'll google him." Shaking my head, I headed home to my laptop. My friend was one bossy woman and wouldn't stop hounding me until I did as she said. I was deep into my online search when a more alert Eric joined me. He sat next to me at the picnic table.

"What are you doing?"

"Googling my absent tenant." I straightened from the keyboard. "He doesn't exist before 2010."

Eric frowned. "That's weird. Are you sure? There must be thousands of Ted Smiths."

"There are, but only one with his social security number." I turned my screen around to show the man's social media page. "Look familiar?"

He glanced from the screen to me. "That's the dead guy."

"Yep. Once again, the resident of house number ten is part of a mystery." I glanced toward the house. "I think it's cursed."

"I'm starting to wonder about this whole place." His eyes twinkled as he met my gaze. "Of course, none of this happened until you took over."

"Hey. Things were stolen before I arrived on the scene."

"Barely. You'd already accepted the job." He laughed, then sobered when his gaze fell on the laptop again. "I guess we'd better let Davis know we have the man's name."

"Since he hasn't existed for long, do you think he's in witness protection?"

"That's a fair assumption." He dialed Davis on his cell phone, putting him on speaker when the detective answered. Eric told him of how I'd found the man's identity.

"It was actually Mags's idea," I said.

"I thought you were going to stay out of this one," Davis said.

"I only wanted to know more about my tenant and why he hasn't moved in." I crossed my arms. "I can't help if he's also the murder victim."

"This could be dangerous, CJ. I'm serious about you not getting involved. I'll do some research on my end." Click.

"He didn't sound surprised about the man's identity, did he? It was as if he already knew." Oh. He'd already run prints off the finger Caper found through the database. I was definitely staying out of all this. On the crime shows I enjoyed watching, witness protection meant the mob was involved. I did not want to mess with those guys.

Chapter Three

"You don't say. Well." Mags's brows rose to her hairline. "Witness protection." She plopped back into her easy chair. Her calico cat jumped into her lap. "This is exciting, even for Heavenly Acres."

"Number ten is vacant again." I sighed. Most of our residents were homeowners, renting only the space their house sat on, but I had rentals that stayed full most of the year, dropping off during the winter months. Number ten, though. That one was more like a hotel than a home.

I stood. "I'm going to check the place out on the inside." Smith had probably never entered, but I had more curiosity in my petite body than ten cats.

"I'll go with you." Mags patted her pocket. "Still don't go anywhere without my Taser."

"Don't let Eric know." I chuckled remembering the time he'd startled Mags and she'd tased him. He'd not been a happy park ranger when he struggled to his feet.

I retrieved the key under the mat of number ten and opened the door. The place had that unlived-in smell. No furniture, no personal belongings.

"Out."

I shrieked and whirled, coming face-to-face with Davis.

Mags already had her Taser in her hand.

Davis pointed at her. "You zap me, and you'll find yourself in jail faster than a duck jumps on a June bug."

"Why do we have to get out?" I crossed my arms and narrowed my eyes. "I need to make sure the place is ready to rent."

"Nope. It's a potential crime scene." He motioned his head toward the door.

"The man never set foot inside."

"We don't know that. Get. Out."

I huffed and stomped outside to see rookie officer—and now one of my closest friends—Ann Lowery stringing yellow crime-scene tape across the tiny porch. She gave me a wry grin. "Sorry."

"It isn't your fault." I glared over my shoulder at Davis. Ann became my temporary bodyguard during the last adventure. I was pretty sure she wasn't keen on repeating the process since I tended to anger murderers and the police chief by following every clue with dogged determination.

"You aren't getting involved in this, are you?" She asked.

"There's nothing to get involved in. Other than the man signing a lease, his death has nothing to do with me."

She didn't look convinced. "Remember that, okay?"

Mags, who had remained uncharacteristically silent, spoke up. "If evidence presents itself, we can't turn away and ignore it."

"You don't have to go looking for it." Ann frowned. "If you do discover something, as CJ did with the man's identity, you let a law-enforcement officer know. That's it."

Amber, Mags's granddaughter and Davis's girlfriend, joined us. "Is Bill making things difficult again?"

Mags nodded. "I don't know why you can't convince that man to give us special privileges. It's as if you aren't even trying."

Rather than be put out by her grandmother's words, Amber laughed. "He has a job to do and trying to keep the two of you safe makes it harder. Just because we're seeing each other doesn't mean he's allowed to tell me about his cases."

"It isn't my fault my dog keeps bringing me clues. It's my job as a citizen to see justice done." True, but the responsibility of following those clues rested solely on my shoulders and on the urging of Mags.

"You watch too many crime shows," Amber said. "The two of you are not partners in crime-solving."

"Oh, yes we are." Mags gave her "the look." "We've been responsible in one way or another for bringing down two criminals. We aren't talking about the stealing-doughnuts-kind-of-criminals either. I'm talking about chase-you-through-the-woods-and-try-to-kill-you type. I think that makes us highly capable partners."

Mags was not making things any better considering Davis had come outside in time to hear her latest statement. He scowled and stood next to Amber. "Maybe I should arrest you and save myself a headache."

"On what grounds?" Mags lifted her chin.

Seriously, watching the two of them butt heads had to be the world's best entertainment. Amber must have thought so, too because although she wore her nursing scrubs, she didn't seem to be in a hurry to leave. Instead, she watched the proceedings with a big grin on her face.

"Bill has the patience of a saint," she said.

"Really?" My brows lowered. "He doesn't seem to have any in my opinion."

"Of course, he does." She glanced at me. "If he didn't, you and Mags would've been arrested multiple times by now. He told me once that the small jail in town wasn't built to house both of you."

I wasn't sure how to take that. Did he mean there weren't enough cells or that we were troublemakers? "Not even Mags and I could escape a jail cell." I rolled my eyes.

Having finished sparring with Mags, Davis marched toward his squad car, Amber following. He gave her a quick kiss and opened the car door, then glared at us. "I'm serious, ladies." He climbed into the driver's seat and drove away.

Amber tossed a wave and left in her own car.

"Serious about what?" I asked.

"Staying away from number ten until they've removed the tape."

Ann came from around the house. "Doesn't look as if anyone has lived here in weeks."

"That's what I tried to tell Davis." I sighed. "How long until I can rent this place? Who do I give the deposit to?"

"His estate, I guess."

"Did he have one?" My eyes widened. "I guess I could just not cash the check, and the money will stay in his account."

Her eyes brightened. "You haven't cashed it yet?"

"I always wait until the person moves in."

"Give it to me. Maybe the bank will know something more about this man." She followed Mags and me to my house.

I reached into a folder on the wall above my table and pulled out the check. "I'm not sure what a bank account will tell you. Wouldn't you find more information on his phone?"

"You have his phone?" Her mouth dropped open.

"No, I'm thinking out loud. I do have his cell phone number on his application. You can obtain the records, right?" I handed her the application. "This is all I have on the man. Good luck. Can you tell me who he was?"

"Sorry. You know the answer to that." She flashed a grin and strolled out the door.

"Tell me you made copies of those things," Mags said.

"Of course, I did. I'm supposed to send a copy

to the owner of this community." I grinned and wiggled my brows. "But, we're not getting involved."

"Nope." Her smile widened. "Wouldn't even know where to start on this one. Ted Smith didn't exist before he was killed."

"Yep. We don't know anything about the real man."

"So now what?"

I shrugged. "No idea." This wasn't like finding a necklace buried under my house or Caper bringing me a leather pouch of diamonds. This time, we really had nothing to go on, not even the finger.

"We do know what he looks like," Mags pointed out. "Maybe we can find out something in the archived newspapers at the library. If he was in witness protection, there had to be a reason."

"You are one smart cookie." I locked Caper in the house and led Mags to my little red Prius.

"What we need," Mags said, clicking her seatbelt into place, "is for your nosy dog to find us a clue."

That would help immensely. "Right. We need more body parts. Find those and we might figure out why the man was killed. All the evidence in one place and all."

"Would be convenient."

Which meant not likely, unless whoever killed Smith was stupid. I didn't think we'd get that lucky.

Chapter Four

Our town library was small, but it did keep all local papers online. Score one for us.

Mags headed straight for the computers, but I decided to question the librarian first. One thing small towns were known for was knowing everyone else's business.

"Good morning," I glanced at the name plate on the desk, "Alice. I'm hoping you can answer a couple of questions for me."

The elderly woman smiled. "I'll certainly try."

"It's kind of a strange request." I leaned on the counter.

"Honey, you wouldn't believe the questions we're asked."

"I'm wondering whether you can remember anything in the news about someone turning evidence against some powerful people."

"Like the mob or a politician?" She wrinkled her brow.

"It was most likely during the last ten years." Considering the dead guy looked to be in his late thirties to early forties, I hoped I was making a good assumption. Going through ten years of newspapers would take a long time. Hopefully, she could narrow it down for us.

"I do remember something, but it wasn't one of our residents." She headed for a computer on the other end of the counter. "A neighboring city had a bit of trouble with drugs, if I recall. They arrested someone, and he spilled his guts. Here are the last five years. Do a search for drug evidence, arrest, etc. I bet you'll find what you're looking for. I'm surprised you don't remember this."

"I didn't watch the news much." Grams said the news depressed her and turned it off after the evening weather forecast. "Thanks." I perched on a stool after she went to help another customer.

"I can't find anything." Mags stood behind me.

"Alice said it happened about five years ago."

"Hm. Why don't I remember?"

I shrugged. "I didn't either. My guess is there wasn't a big enough fuss made."

"Why wouldn't there be? This would be big news around here."

"That's what I'm trying to find out. Hush." I scanned the articles that came up when I typed in *drug bust*. Nothing to help us there. I typed in *drug dealer turned state evidence*. Bingo. A grainy newspaper photo of the dead guy, only this time he wore a prison uniform and handcuffs.

The article went on to say that Robert Evans, small-time drug dealer, promised to reveal the names of those higher up the chain in order to receive a lighter sentence. After five years, the man disappeared. That must be when he became Ted Smith. Only thing was, someone knew his new identity and made the man pay for turning traitor.

"Those are some bad people," Mags said. "I agree. Let's stay out of this one."

"That's the smartest thing you've said in a long time." I printed out the article and folded it in my purse. "Want to go to lunch?"

"Absolutely."

We headed toward the door, almost bumping into a man just a few feet away. "Excuse me." I frowned and stepped around him, holding the door open for Mags.

We walked down Main Street, a mere few blocks at the end of a T-junction, and entered a café that served everything from American to Mexican food. The place was already packed, and we chose a table in the back.

I ordered a chef salad while Mags ordered the special—chicken fried steak and mashed potatoes. "How do you stay so thin?" I asked.

"A good metabolism. You should try eating more. You're too skinny."

"I've always been thin no matter what I eat. I happen to like salads. I ate a huge burger just the other day."

"Wow." She smirked and reached for her glass of sweet tea. "Isn't that the man from the library? Don't look."

"How am I supposed to answer your question if I don't look?" I glanced behind me. Two tables over was the man we'd almost run into. "Yes, that's him, but it doesn't mean anything. This is a popular place to eat, and it's a small town."

"Then why is he staring at us?"

"He's probably wondering where he's seen us before. Stop staring back."

"What if he's following us?"

"Stop reading into things that aren't there. Why in the world would he be following us?"

She looked at me as if I'd grown a third eye over my nose. "He could have overheard us talking and knows we're looking into the death of Robert Evans."

"Shh. Don't say that name out loud. He no longer exists, remember? Besides, why follow us to the library? He has no idea who we are." I glanced back to see the man still looking our way. Our gazes met for a second, then he looked at his menu. "See? He's only here to eat."

"I don't believe in coincidences." She straightened when the server set the plate in front of her. "Everyone knows who you are. Your face has been in the newspaper twice."

I sighed and poured ranch dressing over my salad. Maybe if I dropped the subject, she would. I didn't want to talk about our findings in public regardless. Whether I planned to pursue information on Ted Smith was my business. But if it got back to Davis, even if my search was out of curiosity, he'd be livid.

"You've done a good job with Heavenly Acres," Mags said. "The residents seem happy. The security cameras make them feel safer. Everyone keeps their lots tidy, even Doris Schultz. She keeps her curtains closed so I can't tell if she's hoarding again, but the outside isn't cluttered."

I narrowed my eyes. "You're spying on everyone?"

"I told you I patrol every evening. It's my exercise." She waved her fork at me. "It wouldn't hurt for you to venture out after dark. That's when everything happens. Lucy Flower stills spends a lot of time with Dave Lincoln in number three, leaving her brood in Rose's care."

"As long as the children aren't in danger, it's none of my business. Don't be the neighborhood busybody."

She continued as if I hadn't said a word. "Danny still sneaks out at night and walks with me, which is the only reason I haven't told his mother on him. The dear boy thinks I need protection. Davis is at Amber's at least twice a week."

"All right. What do you know about me and Eric?"

She laughed. "You two are boring. The one and only time he spent the night, he slept on the sofa."

I'd be making sure my curtains were fully closed from now on. "You're incorrigible."

"I see and hear things. It's for the good of the community." She resumed eating.

When we'd finished, I paid for both our lunches. Outside, the temptation to visit the flea market next door lured me. The only thing keeping me from going inside was the fact I had nowhere to put anything. My tiny house was comfortable and uncluttered. Just the way I liked it. Still, one never knew what treasures they could find.

Mags made the decision for me and entered the market, sending me a questioning look through the glass door. I followed.

As I turned to enter the first stall, I glanced back to see the man from the library and café staring at us through the window. Mags was right. He was following us.

Chapter Five

I stared back, letting him know I knew he was there. That's what they said on the crime shows. Let the suspect know you noticed them. Don't be a blind victim.

As if I didn't have a care in the world, I browsed the antiques and junk, searching for an item I couldn't live without. Hopefully, I'd find something pretty that could also be used as storage. In a tiny house, everything needed to serve more than one purpose.

In the back of the shop, I discovered a rectangle chest and an octagonal one. They'd be perfect to replace the cheap coffee table I had and provide much-needed storage for blankets.

"How do you plan on getting those home?" Mags frowned. "They won't fit in the Prius."

"I'll have Eric return with me later." I paid for my purchase and waited while the clerk put a sold sign on them. Then I eyed the large bag in Mags's hands. "What did you get? Your house is already bursting."

"Figurines of cats. I love them." With a hitch of her chin, she marched out the front door.

Soon, she wouldn't be able to talk about Mrs. Schultz because her house would be as bad as the hoarder's. I climbed into the driver's seat. "Do you need to go anywhere else before we head home?"

"The police station."

"Why?" My mouth dropped opened.

"Because the staring man is sitting in his car two spots behind us. My guess is he wants to see where we go. Home is definitely not the place we should go."

"Great." I turned the key in the ignition. "We'll have to tell Davis why the man is following us. He's going to throw us in jail."

"He can't arrest us for finding public information online that anyone can if they look hard enough." She clicked her seatbelt into place. "Drive naturally."

I pulled out of the parking spot and wandered around town. The dark sedan followed. Why did they always drive dark sedans? Without a doubt the man was following us, so I turned into the police-station parking lot and watched as the man drove by. "Good. We don't have to go in."

"What are you going to say to Davis later?" She motioned out the window. "He's standing on the steps."

I stuck my head out the window. "Engine light flickered, but it's off now. No worries." I waved and drove away.

"You're a terrible liar." Mags shook her head. "He's going to tell Eric who will then take a look at your car and find out nothing is wrong."

"I'll tell Eric the truth." I drove home, glancing in my rearview mirror. It wasn't until I turned into the community that I spotted the dark sedan again. Great. Now he knew where we lived.

Deciding not to tell Mags in case she got scared, I dropped her off at her house and went to mine to fetch my dog. Caper might be small, but she'd let me know if anyone was around who wanted to harm me. I was tempted to call Eric but chose not to. He had work to do and couldn't come to my aid every time I thought I might be in trouble. He'd never get any work done.

Leaving Caper off her leash, I took a seat on my porch so I could keep a close eye on the entrance to Heavenly Acres. Thirty minutes passed with no sign of the sedan. I laughed at my foolishness. The man obviously wasn't following us because here I sat in plain sight.

Roy stopped his golf cart next to my house. "We've got a leak in number ten."

"Can't you fix it?"

"I wasn't sure whether I could with the crime-scene tape up, but the place is going to be ruined if we don't get inside."

"All right." I hopped down and into the cart. "I'll take full responsibility. Let's go."

He drove to number ten. I ducked under the tape and unlocked the front door. Water spewed from under the kitchen sink. Sloshing my way through two inches of water, I tried turning the faucet. It was already off. “Come on in, Roy.”

He splashed to my side and knelt in the water to peer under the sink. “Looks like a loose fitting.”

“A lot of water for a fitting.”

“The seal is cracked.”

“Which means nothing to me.” I folded my arms and leaned against the wall, contemplating the damage to the building. The floor would need replacing. I could only hope the walls were still in good shape.

“What on God’s green earth?” Roy held up a tube. “This was jammed in the pipe.”

Growing smarter about evidence handling with every mystery, I held the tube with the hem of my shirt and removed the lid. Rolled papers filled the inside. I pulled them out. My heart dropped to my knees. Two pages of names. “I need to go. Turn off the water and get out of this house. You were never here. Understand?”

“What’s going on?”

“It’s best you don’t know. Not a word.” I rushed outside and called Davis. If my suspicions were correct, I held the list of names Smith had given to the authorities. This was one thing I wouldn’t keep a copy of. If only I could forget the few names I did read. If anyone on that list found out I had it…I didn’t want to contemplate the danger. With a call to Caper, I locked us both in my house.

A loud pounding on the front door fifteen minutes later had me screaming like a victim in a horror movie. Caper barked loud enough to burst eardrums.

"CJ," Davis yelled through the door.

I yanked the door open. "You scared me half to death."

"You will be dead if you found what I think you found." His eyes flashed. "Why were you in that house?"

"I told you a pipe burst." I handed him the tube I'd slipped into a paper sack. "I promise I did not make copies."

"Finally, you have some sense." He exhaled and rested a hand on my shoulder. "Ann will be staying with you again, and she's not happy. She said she's a police officer, not a bodyguard. Why can't you stay out of trouble?"

"I didn't go looking for this. The real question here is why is it always number ten?"

"What?" He scowled.

"Nothing." I fell onto the sofa. "When is Ann coming?"

"Within the hour."

All I'd wanted when I'd taken the job at Heavenly Acres was a peaceful life where I could worry about no one but myself for a change. Instead, it was the exact opposite. My life was definitely different than when I'd cared for Grams. I almost preferred that boring, simple life.

"Are you about to cry?" Davis paled. "Do I need to call someone?"

I laughed, pushing back tears. "I'm fine, don't be such a wuss."

"Okay."

"I didn't ask for this. All I wanted was a day off."

"I have no idea what you're talking about. I'm calling Eric." He rushed outside.

I sighed and sagged against the back of the sofa feeling a horrible sense of déjà vu. I'd been in this same predicament a month ago. In danger and needing a bodyguard.

Davis stuck his head inside. "Eric is on his way." "I'm leaving. Lock the door. Don't open for anyone other than Eric or Ann."

"Or me." Mags squeezed past him. "What's going on?"

"Ann is coming."

"Oh." Her eyes widened. "What did you do?"

I told her about the tube.

"Let me see it."

"Davis has it."

"Didn't you make copies?"

I shook my head. "Not this time."

"Have I taught you nothing?"

"This isn't something we should be involved in."

"We didn't ask to find that finger or that tube." She sat next to me. "I'm going to buy a gun."

"Heaven forbid," Ann said, entering the house. "The world's not ready for that."

"Sorry." I shrugged. "I know you're trying to make detective, and babysitting me interferes with that."

"Oh, well. I do wish you had a more comfortable sofa, though."

"You can sleep with me. The bed is big enough." I blinked back the tears I refused to release. Now was not the time to let my emotions run free. I had to be strong, cautious…resigned to the fact I was neck deep in another murder case.

Chapter Six

"I want number ten off this land." I glanced from Mags to Ann. "Do you think the owner will understand?"

"No," Mags said. "You're the only one who thinks that house is cursed. It's simply a matter of bad luck and coincidence. Because of the revolving door, it's usually the only house available for a new tenant, thus open for bad guys."

"What are we dealing with?" I asked Ann.

She shrugged one shoulder. "Nothing more than drug lords and gang members."

"Oh, no worries then." I gave a shaky smile. "I'll sleep well at night."

"I didn't let anyone kill you the last time, and I won't let them kill you now." Ann headed up the stairs with a duffel bag.

"I'm still going to buy a gun," Mags leaned over and whispered.

A giggle escaped me despite the severity of the

situation. To distract me further, I opened my laptop and sent the owner a damage report on the flooded tiny house. The floors would need to be replaced. I also told him of the tube hidden in the pipes. Let him decide what to do with the place. Or her. I still wasn't sure who owned Houses, Inc.

A key turned in the lock of the front door. The three of us watched, Ann with her hand on her gun.

"It has to be someone we know," I said. "I don't give out keys willy-nilly."

Eric entered. He scowled at Ann. "This can't be good. Davis said I was needed. What happened?"

All three of us started talking at once.

He held up a hand. "CJ."

I told him what we found at the library, in the plumbing, and of being followed. "Davis thinks I need a bodyguard again."

He plopped down next to me. "It appears you do." His arm went around me, and I laid my head on his shoulder. "CJ should stand for Constant Jeopardy instead of Clarice Josephine."

"That's your real name?" Ann's eyes widened. "You poor thing."

"Why do you think I go by my initials?"

"Instead of talking about trivial things," Mags said, "why aren't we deciding our next step?"

"There is no next step," Eric told her. "You stay out of sight until Davis catches whoever killed that man."

I straightened and frowned. "He might never catch him. These aren't amateurs. I'm not going to be a prisoner in my own home."

"The best defense is offense." Mags crossed

her arms. "I say we lay a trap."

"You aren't the target." I stood. "I've a job to do. Ann will go everywhere I go until those people leave me alone. If I act as if I don't know anything, they'll think I don't and go away." True or not, the thought was what I needed not to crumble into a quivering mass of fear. "Who's hungry? Oh, and I need to go back to the flea market to pick up my chests."

"We could stop at the pizza parlor," Eric suggested. "Give me a couple of minutes to change out of my uniform, and I'll be back to pick y'all up."

Fifteen minutes later, minus Mags who said she'd had enough excitement for one day, we headed back to town. After loading the chests into the back of Eric's jeep, we drove to the one-and-only pizza place in town.

I kept a close watch through the passenger-side mirror and didn't see anything out of the ordinary. Some of the tension left my shoulders, and the pounding in my head subsided. Maybe I could enjoy my supper. I loved pizza, the more meat the better.

We chose a booth in the center of the restaurant. Ann took a seat across from Eric and me where she could have a good view of both doors. She told us it was a "cop thing." I didn't care. My stomach wanted food. The salad at lunch hadn't lasted long enough. So much for eating healthy.

"Do you want me to order a pizza or do you want the buffet?" Eric asked.

"Buffet." I slid from the booth and rushed for

the line of hungry patrons. Grabbing a plate, I got behind a middle-aged woman I'd seen enter the restaurant with two men. All three of them piled their plates high. I hoped they left enough for the rest of us.

When Eric, Ann, and I returned to our seats, the group of three dug into their food in the booth behind us.

"You going to eat all that?" Ann asked. Her plate held two slices, while mine had five.

"I had to nab the dessert pizza before they ran out." I grinned and dug in. "After the day I had, I need nourishment."

"Where do you plan on putting those chests?" Eric asked. "You don't have a lot of room."

"They'll fit and hold lots of stuff." I grinned.

"One of them is big enough to hold you."

We didn't talk about what else I'd done that day. Ann had warned us in the car not to say anything unless we were sure we were alone. I was more than happy to oblige, preferring to pretend none of it happened, including Caper finding that finger.

No one followed us home. More of the day's stress vanished.

Eric led me to our favorite spot by the lake. Caper sniffed around the bushes. Ann watched from the chair on the porch. Close enough to keep an eye on us, but far enough away to give us a little privacy, something we rarely had.

"I think I can count on one hand the times we've been truly alone together," I said, nestling up to him.

"Amazing that we're able to have a relationship at all." He gave me a one-arm hug. "I feel as if someone has lit a courting lamp."

"Chaperones like in the 1800s." I laughed. "Usually it's Mags. At least Ann holds back a bit."

"Hmm." He kissed the top of my head and returned his attention to the lake.

The moon kissed the smooth surface, laying a path of silver. The water looked still enough to walk on, reflecting the trees along the shore as inky shadows. This view and the man next to me were the main reasons I didn't live in Grams's house. I got to see both every day.

Eric's phone rang. He pulled it from the sheath on his belt. "Ranger Drake." He listened for a few minutes, then said, "I'll be right there." He stood and held out his hand to me. "Want to grab Caper and come with me? Robinson said there are some loud campers and they won't listen to him."

"Sure." Yes, sometimes Eric's job interfered with our alone time, but as long as I was with him, I didn't mind.

We took his side-by-side so Ann could squeeze in with us and set off at a quick speed toward the campgrounds. The constant whipping of her head to the left, right, and behind us caused the return of my nerves.

"Calm down. You look suspicious," I said. "You're just a visiting friend, same as before, so stop acting like a cop."

"Right." She slumped in her seat, not doing a very convincing job of disinterest.

Eric pulled up to Robinson's trailer. The tall,

older man unfolded himself from a lawn chair and strolled toward us.

"Thanks, Ranger. Site 103. A bunch of drunken yahoos who won't settle down even though it's after ten p.m." Robinson frowned. "The reservation and posted rules clearly state to be quiet after ten."

"If they won't, I'll give them a ticket." He drove us down the pathway toward the site. Loud music and laughter reached us before the partiers came into sight. He parked behind their truck. "You women stay here." Eric strode to where three young men toasted him with beer cans.

"We've had some complaints, gentlemen. The manager said he's spoken with you several times about quieting down."

"Yeah, so?" One young man tilted his head back, downed the beer, then tossed the can in the fire pit. "We've as much right to have fun as anyone."

"Not at the expense of others. If you don't heed my advice," Eric warned, "I'll have to give you a ticket."

The three drunk men responded with loud obscenities.

Eric wrote out a ticket and handed the paper to them.

One of them slapped it away, then two-hand shoved my man.

Ann put a hand on my shoulder to stop me from jumping out of the vehicle. "I'll handle this." She strode forward and flashed her badge. "Who wants the handcuffs on first because all three of you are going to jail."

I sighed at the crowd that gathered. Ann had just blown her cover.

Chapter Seven

Even with Ann sleeping beside me, I tossed and turned, jumping at every little sound. I'd sit up in bed, check whether Caper was bothered, and lie back down when the dog didn't seem to be on alert. Morning came way too early.

Ann groaned and rolled over. "I feel sorry for your future husband. You toss around more than laundry in a washing machine."

"Nerves." I grabbed my clothes and thundered down the stairs to reach the bathroom first.

Ann followed at a slower clip. "I'll make coffee."

When I emerged from the shower, Ann handed me a cup. I added creamer and headed for the door.

"Where are you going?"

"To let Caper out and have my coffee." I frowned.

"Nope. You stay in the house."

"You'll have to shoot me for that to happen."

Didn't anyone listen when I said I wouldn't become a prisoner in my own home? I opened the door and peered out. Caper dashed between my legs. When she didn't seem disturbed, I moved outside, down the steps, and sat at the picnic table same as every morning. I shot Ann a defiant look when she joined me, daring her to order me back in the house.

"You must have a death wish. There could be a sniper across the lake with you in his scope. Boom. You're none the wiser."

"I want to pretend that nothing is happening. Don't know anything, haven't seen anything, and you're just a friend who also happens to be a cop. That's my story, and I'm sticking to it."

She shrugged. "It's as good as any, I guess. Sorry I blew my cover, but Eric was outnumbered. Not everyone respects the authority of a park ranger."

"I appreciate that." Eric stepped up behind me and placed a tender kiss below my right ear. "Thank you for also wanting to come to my aid," he whispered.

I laughed. "I wouldn't have been much help, since I've never been in a fight in my life."

"It's the thought that counts." He sat next to me.

"Coffee." I jumped up and rushed into the house to make him a cup and refresh mine. I used to always have one ready for him, but a lot of times his job called him away. Now, I waited until he showed up. Same with supper.

Morning java made, I grabbed my laptop and headed back outside to plan my day. I handed Eric his cup and booted my laptop to check emails. The owner said he would send a truck to replace number ten with a new house as soon as the police released it. I also had a reservation for house number twenty starting today. I sent them an affirmative, pleased they paid their deposit upfront and filled out the application.

I did a quick credit check. "I've a new renter arriving this morning, which means I need to head to number twenty and make sure it's ready." It probably only need a cleaning, which Roy's wife, Tammy, would do.

"I'll let you get to it." Eric gave me another kiss. "I'm floating the river today, looking for anything amiss, but I should be back by supper."

"Don't find any dead bodies." I shuddered.

"I don't plan on it." He grinned and headed for his jeep.

"Let's go check out that house." Ann gathered our cups and set them on the porch steps.

I felt sorry for the rookie. Babysitting me was filled with routine and boredom to someone who craved adventure. Which I didn't. Funny how adventure and trouble with a capital T seemed to find me, though. Once it did, I latched on and shook it, trying to rattle loose clues to put an end to it all. Maybe I needed a psychiatrist.

Ann joined me and Caper in the golf cart and we headed for the opposite end of the community. Since I lived in house number one, which Ann thought unsafe considering the circumstances and the close proximity of the gate, house number twenty took five minutes to drive to as the main road curved around the common green area.

"Stop whipping back and forth," I told Ann. "You're making me carsick the way the cart is rocking."

"I need to know what's going on around us every second."

I rolled my eyes. "The only thing I see is the Flower children playing on the playground before the day grows too hot and a couple of joggers enjoying the morning."

"Do they live here?"

"Yes, they live here. Geez." I pulled in front of number twenty, a cute little blue and white house, and parked. "You'll like this one. It's done up rustic."

"I prefer modern."

I shrugged and unlocked the door, stepping into a house paneled in pine. Galvanized steel paneled the walls of the small bathroom. A steel barrel served as a tub. If I hadn't been assigned number one, I would have chosen this one, although I loved my simple home.

Other than a coat of dust over everything, the house was move-in ready. I sent a quick text to Tammy to come clean. I'd escort the new tenant to her home when she arrived.

Ann sighed when I told her we'd be making the rounds of the community. "You just love being out in the open, don't you?"

"Yep. I also want to visit the chapel and make sure no vandals or homeless people messed with anything." The chapel and large illuminated cross had been my first undertaking after accepting the job as overseer, and the cross's intense light helped me escape a gun-wielding murderer.

I drove the full circle, then parked at the path leading past the chapel toward the campgrounds. With the morning sun filtering through the trees, the lake's waves rippling on our left and birds serenading us from above, this was my second favorite place to be. The first was the fallen log at the edge of the lake with Eric's arm around my shoulders.

A soft breeze tickled the back of my neck from my place in front of the double-glass doors. The chapel's peacefulness erased the tension from my shoulders. I stepped inside and took a deep breath, then glanced around. The green of the surrounding foliage filled the glass walls, giving the place a fairyland feel. Ann's voice interrupted.

"Why don't you lock the doors?" Ann asked.

"I want everyone to feel free to enter as needed. It may not be church in the traditional sense in that we don't have a pastor, but it's simply a place to…be. No church should be locked from the people."

"Okay. Ready to head back?"

I glanced at my watch. Nine forty-five. "Yes, the new tenant should be arriving soon."

The woman standing in front of my house looked familiar. When I slid out of the golf cart, it hit me. The woman with the two men in line at the pizza buffet. I thrust out my hand. "CJ Turley. It's nice to meet you."

"Norma Waters." She returned the shake. "My sons are already at the house with the U-Haul. I hope that's all right."

"Of course. Your application said you were the only occupant."

"I am. They're here merely to unload my things. I'm a widow, and the home we used to live in is much too big for little old me."

I could relate. I didn't want to rattle around alone in Grams's house either. "Shall we?"

She joined me in the golf cart, casting a wary eye at Ann in the back. I introduced Ann as my friend who visited me on a regular basis, then drove us to Norma's new home.

Two large men, like muscled bookends, waited in front of the house. A U-Haul sat next by. "These are my sons, Luke and Mark," Norma said. "Handsome, aren't they?"

Not really. Too big and surly, with bushy brows and scowl lines around their mouths. Both wore reflective sunglasses that caused the sun's glare to blind me. "They sure are."

"Boys, this is CJ Turley. She's going to be taking good care of me." Norma joined the men.

I followed and handed her the key. "I hope you're happy here."

She faced me with a smile. "I'm sure I will be." With that, she climbed the porch stairs and unlocked the door, effectively dismissing me. Her sons continued to eye me until I climbed into the cart and drove away.

"I've heard of boys watching out for their mother, but those two take it to a whole other level," Ann said.

"We get all kinds here."

"Are you going to stay safe inside for the rest of the day?"

I exhaled slowly. "I'll be bored stiff."

"Better than stiff in a coffin."

"Fine." I could spend a little time positioning my new chests and organizing my drawers and cupboards. Which took all of an hour. Ugh. I plopped on the sofa and propped my feet on my new chest coffee table, then flipped through channels on the TV.

Ann glanced over from her laptop. "Why don't you read a book?"

"Why don't you?"

"I'm working, trying to find out anything I can about Robert Evans before his arrest."

"I can help with that." I turned off the TV, set my laptop on my lap and turned it on. This would be a lot better than watching television, and I'd be doing something constructive. "You can access places I can't, but I might run across something on social media sites."

"I'll concentrate on databases; you focus on that."

For the next couple of hours, the only sounds were the tapping of our fingers on keyboards and the soft snoring of Caper. Until she barked. I shrieked and almost dropped my laptop.

Ann put a finger to her lips, her other hand on her gun, and waited. A few seconds later a knock sounded on the door. She cracked it open. "Yes?"

"The water isn't working in the house my mother just rented."

Ann glanced over at me. "I thought you

checked everything."

"I didn't turn on the water." I palmed my forehead. "I'll do that right away." What an idiot I was at times. I'd have to check the breaker box, too. "See what happens when I get distracted? I can't do my job when you're rushing me home."

"Pardon me for trying to keep you alive."

"Let's go." I left Caper in the house and walked a few feet away to a small concrete building that held everything needed for plumbing and electricity. The breakers looked good. "We'll have to go to the house to turn on the water."

When we arrived in the golf cart, the two men were carrying in boxes and furniture. I apologized for my oversight and turned on the water, then took a quick peek through the front door at small-scale furniture, a case of diet soda, and plastic bags of groceries.

One of the men spoke with Norma, motioning his head toward the door. "She'll need watching."

Norma nodded. "That's the plan, isn't it? Don't presume to tell me how to run things. You know what happened to Matt."

I stepped off the porch. The wood squeaked under my feet. Norma and Mark spun around and glared. "Water's on." I grinned and darted for the golf cart. *Please, God, don't let them be talking about watching me*. I turned the cart around and sped home.

"What's got you on the run?" Ann cut me a quick glance.

"I overhead them talking about someone needing watching. I was standing on the front porch."

"Were they talking about you?"

I shrugged. "Maybe."

Ann's cop face fell into place. "I'm going to do a background check on your new resident."

Chapter Eight

I didn't know what time Ann finally came to bed, but the first words out of her mouth the next morning were, "Waters is clean. Mother of three boys, widowed, recently sold her house."

"That's good, right?" I glanced up from my cup of coffee.

"Sure." She sounded disappointed. "What's on the agenda for today? Oh, you'll be happy to know I can take down the crime-scene tape. The victim left nothing behind but a couple of fingerprints on the pipes."

So, he had been inside and was killed before moving in the rest of his things. "I'll tell the owner we can switch out the houses." I'd be glad to get rid of the cursed number ten. I'd call the new one, house number ten point two. I sent a quick email to the owner, then answered Ann. "While we wait for the new house to arrive, we make our normal morning rounds, take care of any issues that may rise, then do whatever we want."

"Boring."

"You need a hobby."

"You're my hobby." She scowled into her half-empty cup.

"Go swimming, go for a hike, anything to get out of the house."

"Only if you go."

I finished the last swallow of my coffee. "I didn't plan on doing anything today but chill. It's going to be a scorcher."

"Staying cooped up in your tiny house feels too much like being in a box."

"We can go to the grocery store. I need a few things."

"Great." She sprang to her feet. "Let's make the circle, then head to town. Take your time."

I rolled my eyes at my strung-tight friend, then stood and made my way to the golf cart. I really wanted to relax at home, do a little cleaning, and paint my nails. None of which would appeal to Ann, I was pretty sure.

We saw no sign of Mags in our circuit of the community. Rather strange, in my opinion. I parked in front of her house and hurried up the steps to peer in the window. Her calico cat stared back at me from the back of the sofa. New feline figurines filled the coffee table. I knocked on the door.

A few minutes later, still in her nightgown, a disgruntled Mags opened the door. "What?"

"Are you sick?"

"No. Why?"

"You never sleep this late."

Her brows lowered. "It's not against the law to sleep in once in a while."

I narrowed my eyes. "What were you up to last night?"

"Nothing." She peered around me to where Ann waited in the cart. "Same patrolling as every other night."

"Were you spying on the new tenant?" I crossed my arms. "Ann checked her out. She's clean."

"Those two sons of hers didn't leave until well past midnight. In fact, the three of them huddled around a folding table looking at something for most of the evening."

"So? They're a close family."

"Too close."

I released my breath slowly to keep my composure. "We're headed to town to buy groceries. Do you need anything?"

"Yes. Give me ten minutes to change." She closed the door in my face.

I joined Ann in the cart and drove home to get the Prius. Being an only child, orphaned at a young age, I didn't know whether two adult sons staying at their mother's late was odd or not. It seemed endearing to me. I could only hope if I were blessed with children, they'd want to spend time with me.

Twenty minutes later, Mags arrived wearing a full face of makeup and a fuchsia-colored jogging suit that looked as if it stepped right out of 1976. "Let's go."

"Why are you all dressed up to go to the grocery store?"

“Because there might be single men there. I’ve given up on Robinson showing me any attention.” Mags slid into the front passenger seat. “I’m ready to share my life with a man again.”

Ann snorted. “In that getup?”

Mags glared over her shoulder. “What’s wrong with my outfit? It’s colorful.”

“Yep, people will see you coming a mile away.”

Mags glanced at me. “You should request a new bodyguard. This one lacks manners.”

Laughing, I drove out of the community and toward town. Only ten miles away, we arrived in minutes.

“Here.” Mags handed me a disabled sign. “Left over from my foot surgery.”

“I’m not using that. Someone who needs the spot won’t get it because of our dishonesty.” I pushed her hand away.

“Fine, but I’ll be sticky with sweat before we enter the store.” Mags pouted as I pulled into a parking spot at the end of the filled ones.

“Think of it as exercise to keep your girlish figure in order to catch a man,” Ann said, grinning.

“I get plenty of exercise walking at night.”

Ann paused with her door half open. “You what?”

Uh-oh. “Let’s go. It’s only going to get hotter.” I exited the car.

“What is she talking about?” Ann asked.

“She’s basically the neighborhood watch.”

Ann’s cop face slid into place. “Listen, Mags. I know I’m here to protect CJ, but you’re just as involved as she is. You can't be out wandering the community alone at night."

"I'm not alone. Danny Olson comes with me." Head high, Mags bustled toward the store.

"A teenage boy is not sufficient protection." Ann caught up with her, leaving me to bring up the rear.

The two continued to debate the dangers of the dark until we entered the store. I grabbed a cart and pushed it toward Mags. "Here. Now go shop. Meet us at the front of the store when you're finished." I grabbed another cart for myself.

"It sounds as if you're trying to get rid of me." She plunked her oversized yellow purse in the seat. "Fine by me. I can't deal with Ann right now." She stormed down the cereal aisle.

I glanced at Ann. "You have to handle Mags with a gentle hand or you'll get her hackles up. Telling her she can't do something only makes her want to do it more."

"Like you?" She raised her eyebrows.

My breath released in a huff. "Get whatever you want. I'm buying. Just remember the space constraints." Although I had a full-size refrigerator, cabinet space was in short supply.

Ann added a soft drink she liked and some flavored water, but she spent her time surveying whoever came down the aisle we shopped in. I moved from dry foods to meats, to freezer, to produce, adding to the cart what I thought the two of us—and occasionally, Eric—would eat for the week. I didn't worry about running out. The store wasn't so far that I couldn't make another run in a few days.

I turned the corner to see Mags laughing and grinning at the man we'd seen following us. She caught sight of me and waved me over. "CJ, meet Larry Acres."

"Why were you following us?" Might as well get straight to the point.

"I thought I recognized this woman here. Turns out I did. We went to school together a long, long time ago." His gaze settled gently on my friend.

"Not so long ago," Mags said, giving him a gentle swat on the arm. "Don't wait for me, CJ. Larry's taking me to lunch, then he'll bring me home."

I gripped her arm and dragged her a few feet away. "Are you sure? You don't know this man."

She yanked free. "Sure, I do. We went to school together. He signed my yearbook. I'll show it to you later. Now don't embarrass me." She made a shooing motion with her hands.

"Don't worry," Ann said low enough Mags couldn't hear. "I'll do a background check on him."

"Good, but nothing had better happen to my friend." I strode away, pushing the cart with more force than necessary and knocked over a display of toilet paper. I glanced back to see Mags staring with wide eyes and a red face. Oops. I'd embarrassed her.

I tossed a sheepish grin and started restacking the rolls of paper until a stock boy told me he'd handle it. Not wanting to cause any more trouble, I finished my shopping, then headed for the register in the front of the store.

At the next register, Mags giggled at everything Larry said. The man looked too nice to be trusted. In the crime shows, the bad guy was always the least likely person to commit the deed.

"Stop shooting daggers at him," Ann said. "Remember what you told me about Mags. Think of her as a teenage girl whose mother doesn't like the boy she has a crush on."

Right. I'd have to let nature run its course. "I'm going to keep a close eye on those two."

"You and me both."

Outside the store, a young man and her son picked up a puppy from a cardboard box. "Free to a good home."

"What kind of dog?" My heart leaped.

"Lab."

I hadn't forgotten Eric's dream dog, so I peered into the box. "I'd like the brown one if it's a girl."

"It is." The boy handed me the puppy.

"I know you said free, but here's ten dollars." I handed him the money and nuzzled the puppy under my chin. Caper would be so jealous.

With a spring in my step, I headed for my car, letting Ann push the cart. I couldn't wait to see Eric's face when I handed over Hershey. "Oh, you're such a sweetie." The puppy licked me in the face in response.

A sheet of paper fluttered on the windshield of my car, held in place by the wiper. "I hate advertisements on my window." I'd driven off plenty of times, only to have to stop somewhere and remove one because I hadn't noticed it at first.

I put the puppy in the back seat, the flier in the

front, turned on the air conditioner so the car would cool off, and helped Ann load the groceries in the trunk. By the time we finished, my shirt stuck to my back with perspiration. I slid into the driver's seat, shoving aside the paper, and clicked my seatbelt into place.

Ann did the same, then glanced at the paper. "What's this?" Her eyes widened and she turned it around so I could see.

Written in bold, black letters were the words, *Get your nose out of what doesn't concern you or have it cut off.*

My hand went to my nose as if someone had already nabbed it. I swallowed past the lump in my throat.

Chapter Nine

"See?" Mags glared the next morning when I told her about the note left on my car. "It couldn't have been Larry. He was in the store with me."

"He could have left it before entering the store."

"Why are you so dedicated to the fact that Larry is the one who murdered that guy?" Her eyes glimmered.

"Because he followed us."

"I told you why." She sniffed and transferred her attention to Ann. "Do you think he's the killer?"

Ann shrugged. "I don't know anything at this point. Davis will have the note analyzed and let me know if he finds out anything we need to know. I do agree with CJ that even though Mr. Acres claims he recognized you, it is strange he followed you to so many places."

"Which means we know nothing," I muttered,

then brightened as Eric strolled toward us not wearing his uniform. Wonderful. We could spend the day together.

"Good morning." He bent down and kissed me.

"That's all I want, CJ." Mags nodded at us. "A man who adores me like Eric does you."

"What's this?" Eric straddled the bench.

I filled him in on yesterday's happenings. "It's not that I want Larry to be guilty. I'm just not convinced yet he's as innocent as he wants us to believe he is."

"It is better to err on the side of caution." He patted Mags's hand. "If he's a nice guy, time will tell."

"I'm not going to stop seeing him. Oh, there he is to take me to breakfast." She tossed me a defiant look and strode toward Larry's forest-green Camry. He waved and drove out the gate as a dark blue Ford truck pulled in and drove to number twenty. Right behind them was a tow truck.

"Grand Central Station," I said.

The tow truck parked in front of number ten, backed up to the hitch, and a man climbed out and hooked the house to the truck. Then he left. Later a pink and white tiny house replaced the previous one, just like that.

"It would be nice to be told when these things are happening. I am the overseer." I twisted my lips.

"Who in their right mind wants to live in a pastel pink house?" Ann shuddered. "You might want to have Roy paint it a different color."

"Later." I smiled and headed for the house, returning a minute later with a squirming Hershey in my arms. I handed her to Eric. "Meet your new girlfriend, Hershey."

"What's this?" He grinned, his eyes wide. "Where in the world am I to keep her? Look at her feet. She'll be huge."

"In your house. Take her with you when you go to work. She'll get her exercise that way."

He laughed as the puppy lapped his face. "This is the sweetest thing." He took my hand and pulled me close for a kiss. "Thank you. I'll take her with me on my rounds, but you're my number-one girlfriend. This little beauty has to remain number two."

"I'm going to be sick." Ann rolled her eyes. "You sometimes forget I'm here, don't you?"

"No." I laughed. "I pretend you aren't."

"Fair enough." She grinned when Hershey leaped from Eric's arms and bounded across the table. "You are a cutie, even though you whined all night."

"What do you want to do today?" Eric's warm gaze fell on me.

"I'm up for anything. There's nothing pressing on my to-do list."

"Let's act like a normal couple."

"And?"

"Go to the movies. It's going to be hot today. Grab lunch somewhere." His look grew serious. "Act as if you didn't get a threat to cut off your cute little nose."

"Sounds like a great plan." I felt my nose. Yep, still there. "We might want to stop at the store to pick up a dog crate. She didn't stay in the cardboard box last night and left me some presents on the floor."

"Great." He scooped up the puppy. "Let me put her in my bathroom, and I'll be back to pick you two up."

I darted into my house to change and put on a dab of makeup. In a pair of white capris and an ice-blue blouse that matched my eyes, I locked Caper in the house and waited outside with Ann.

"I'm sorry if I'm cramping your love life," she said. "I know you'd prefer a day with Eric alone."

"No worries. You can sit two rows back at the theater." I flashed her a grin and rested my hand on her arm. "You're doing your job, Ann."

"Right." She returned my smile. "If I don't keep you alive, you won't ever have that alone time you crave."

Good point. Compromising my love of romantic comedies and Eric's penchant for adventure movies, we chose a romantic adventure. I picked seats in the top row center while Ann sat two rows in front of us. Eric waited in line for popcorn and sodas.

I scrutinized every person who came into the theater. No one brought undue attention. Most glanced at the top row and frowned to see the best seats in the house taken, but their stares didn't linger. Except for Mags's. With an angry glance at me, she chose two seats in front of Ann. Every few seconds, she'd toss me another glimpse over her shoulder.

It bothered me to see her so put out, but I had her safety in mind. I prayed she wouldn't let her desire to be loved blind her to danger.

"Why so serious?" Eric asked, handing me a diet soda before taking his seat next to me. He set the large bucket of popcorn in my lap.

"I'm sad that Mags is mad at me." My throat clogged.

"She'll get over it. Don't mention Larry again unless Ann's search digs up something troublesome." He grabbed a handful of popcorn. "I hope you like butter. It's loaded."

"Yum." I tossed a few pieces in my mouth. "I'll try not to say anything more. Have you heard from Davis about the note left on my car?"

"He's looking into it."

"That tells me nothing."

Eric chuckled and settled in his seat as the lights dimmed. He held my hand, giving it a gentle squeeze. "Relax and enjoy the movie. Let all that other stuff go for a while."

Amazingly enough, I did. I laughed, ate popcorn, rested my head on Eric's shoulder during the sappy parts of the movie, and forgot everything else. When the movie ended, Eric grabbed my hand and led me out of the theater, Ann right behind us.

I blinked against the harsh lights of the lobby. The fire alarm blared. I shrieked and jumped back.

The crowd panicked, rushing toward the exits like a tsunami. My hand was ripped from Eric's and I was carried away by the wave. Being petite, I couldn't see over most of the people's heads to locate my friends.

An arm snagged around my waist. I smiled, believing Eric had found me until a hand clamped over my mouth and someone dragged me into a dark theater. I kicked and screamed, fighting against my assailant. From the way he lifted me off my feet, the man must be huge. His hand slipped from my mouth and circled my throat, squeezing until colored spots appeared in front of me. Then as quick, he let me go.

I fell to the floor, my eyes drifting closed. My last thought was about the floor below me. What sort of sticky mess was I lying in?

"I found her." Mags patted my cheek.

"Ow." I shoved her hand away and bolted to a seated position. I put a hand to my aching throat.

"CJ." Eric knelt beside me. "What happened?"

"Someone dragged me in here and choked me. What am I sitting in?" I glanced at the multi-colored carpet, then at the red stain on my white capris.

"Come on." He helped me to my feet. "Let's go outside and call the police."

"Where's the fire?"

"Obviously a diversion to separate us," Ann said. "Very effective. I'm sorry, CJ."

"I'm more curious about why the man didn't kill me. Yes, it was a man. A strong, muscled one. He tossed me around like I didn't weigh anything."

Outside, Eric set me down on a concrete bench circling an oak tree. "Don't move. I'm calling Davis."

Mags handed me a cold soda. "For your throat."

At least she wasn't mad at me anymore. "Thanks." The cool liquid soothed my throat on the way down. "Where's Larry?"

"He was with me the whole time." She glowered.

"I'm not insinuating anything. He isn't as big as the man who attacked me. I don't want you to be alone is all." I spotted Larry watching from the shade of the building, then my gaze wandered over the people in front of the theater, searching for a man big enough to be my attacker. "How did you find me?"

"When we came outside and you weren't anywhere to be seen," Ann said, "we split up and searched the theater. It didn't take long to determine there was no fire and something had happened to you."

"Well, you'd better figure it out." My mild-mannered park ranger paced the sidewalk, a vein throbbing in his forehead. "She could have died today." He pressed the off button on his phone rather hard, then shoved it into his pocket. Taking a deep breath, Eric returned to my side. "Ready? We're going to urgent care to have your throat checked. Then, if you're up to it, we're going to continue our normal day as a dating couple." Jaw set, he held out his hand.

I slipped mine in his. He gently helped me to my feet. From the rigid line of his shoulders, I'm surprised he didn't yank me up. "We don't have to continue the day."

"Yes, we do." Keeping a firm grip on my hand, he told the others they were coming to lunch with us because there was safety in numbers. "I agree with CJ. No hiding."

"What changed your mind?" I glanced at his

red face.

"We need to draw those people out and put them behind bars so life can continue peacefully."

Mags laughed. "It never has been peaceful around CJ. What makes you think it ever will be?"

Concern etched Larry's face. "Are you saying that Clar…CJ is always in danger?"

I caught the slip of his tongue. I narrowed my eyes. "How do you know my real name is Clarice?"

"Mags told me but said you prefer CJ. An honest slip, I assure you."

"It's fine." I waved off his apology and waited for Eric to open the door to his jeep. I slid in the passenger side and clicked my seatbelt into place before resting my head against the headrest. A glimpse in the visor mirror revealed bruises appearing on my pale skin. Wonderful. A daily reminder of what had transpired until they faded.

I straightened at the sight of a large man getting into a jacked-up truck—the type favored by red necks everywhere. Could he be the one? He looked the right size. I hoped he'd turn around so I could see his face. Instead, he disappeared into his truck without glancing back. If he'd been my attacker, he would most likely have been watching to see how I handled his latest warning.

Take that, wherever you are. I won't run screaming into the night. Instead, I'll chase you down with all the tenacity of a pit bull.

Eric gripped my hand. "I know what you're thinking. We'll do this together."

"We all will," Mags said from the back seat. "No one can stand against the Fabulous Five."

I closed my eyes. Larry wasn't going anywhere anytime soon.

Chapter Ten

After the doctor declared no permanent harm had been done to my throat and ordered a diet of soft foods for a few days, Eric decided ice cream for lunch was what I needed. I didn't complain and ordered a strawberry milkshake, then slid into a booth by a large window.

"I wish you didn't always choose a window seat." Ann sat across from me. "Makes you an easy target."

I scowled. "It didn't make any difference that I was in a crowded theater with my friends and bodyguard, now did it?" I took a long drag on my straw. The cool smoothness of the milk shake soothed a throat sorer now than right after the attack.

"Shh." Mags and Larry squeezed in next to Ann. "Doctor said to keep talking to a minimum." She patted my hand. "I know how hard that will be for you."

I rolled my eyes and kept sucking down my shake. I could be quiet if I had to.

Eric slid into the booth beside me. “Milton will meet us at the house to take your report. I’ll text him when we’re on our way.”

“I bet you have them on speed dial by now,” Larry said. “Mags filled me in on all that has happened since CJ arrived at Heavenly Acres.”

“Unfortunately.” Eric dug into his banana split. “We’ll cut the day short and take CJ home to rest.”

My shoulders slumped. Was it too much to ask for a day alone with Eric without someone trying to kill me?

“Are you okay?” Eric’s brow creased.

I nodded. “Sad the day has to end this way.”

“Me too.” He gave me a warm-armed hug. “We’ll sit out by the lake this evening, just the two of us.”

“And Ann.”

“I’ll stay back,” Ann said. “But not too far.”

I sighed and returned to my shake. When we’d finished, Mags and Larry headed for his Camry while the rest of us climbed into Eric’s jeep. I sat up straighter in my seat when we passed Grams’s house. “Stop here.” When he did, I hopped out.

“Whose place is this?” Ann shoved her door open to follow me.

“My grandmother’s. Well, mine now.” I strolled up a brick pathway overgrown with grass and weeds. Withered flowers filled the large cement planters. A morning glory vine still grew healthy along a trellis. Grams had loved its bright purple blossoms. I needed to take better care of the place.

"This house looks lonely," Ann said. "Why don't you live here?"

"I'm not ready to. Besides, I love my tiny house and my job." I removed a key from a plaster frog and unlocked the door. Rather than enter the house, I peered into the dim recess of the living room.

Dust covered every surface. Sheets hid the faded flowered sofa and armchair. Yes, the house looked lonely. I coughed as I breathed in the mustiness of the empty house. Pain ripped through my throat.

"Come on." Eric gently pulled me away. "You can come back when you're in the right health to tackle things here."

I nodded and stepped back, locking the door and pocketing the key. I'd be back soon to decide what to do with the house.

"Would you consider renting the place to me?" Ann asked back in the jeep. "I'm in an apartment right now and would love to live in that cute little house."

My eyes widened and I turned to face her. "Really?"

She nodded. "I promise I'd take good care of it."

Tears filled my eyes. Her offer was an answer to prayer. "I'd love that. We'll go back and clear out personal things in a few days. Then, when you aren't my babysitter anymore, you can move in. It's fully furnished, but I can store the furniture."

"No, my apartment is furnished, so I don't have anything to bring." She smiled and sat back.

Something good came out of the day after all. I flashed a grin at Eric and released a long, tension-releasing breath.

Milton was sitting at the table in front of my house when we pulled up. “Hey, rookie,” he said to Ann. “How’s the babysitting? Glad it’s you again and not me. CJ isn’t the easiest person to watch.”

“I snuck out one time.” I sat across from him while Eric went to fetch Hershey.

“And almost got yourself killed and me fired.” He tapped a pen on a clipboard. “You know the drill. Tell me what happened.”

I told what I knew, and Ann filled in the blanks. So much for limiting my talking. I’d done nothing but talk all day.

“Has Davis found out anything?” Ann asked.

Milton glanced at me, then at her. “Nope.”

“Why is it that any finding of anything comes from me?” I crossed my arms.

“We can’t tell you if we do know anything,” he said. “If I have information, I’ll give it to Officer Lowery here, not you.” He motioned for Ann to go with him as he headed to his squad car. They conversed for a bit, then Ann returned.

“Don’t ask. I won’t tell.” She pressed her lips together.

“Must be bad.” I pushed to my feet and let Caper out. When Eric returned, the two dogs wrestled under the table, making enough noise to make me think they were tearing each other apart.

I propped my chin on my hands and stared across the lake. A few campers strolled along the water’s edge, a man fished from the pier, children raced in and out of the water. Peaceful, serene, often hiding secrets.

Enough feeling sorry for myself. I had a very large, very dangerous man to catch. I ran through my mind what I knew, which wasn't much. My attacker was big and strong. We had a dead man who had been in witness protection for turning state's evidence against a drug lord, whose identity had not been revealed in the newspaper article. I wasn't so naïve that I didn't know people made meth and grew marijuana up in the hills. What if the very people we were searching for lived on the mountain that rose behind Blue Lake and Heavenly Acres?

"What are you thinking?" Eric threw a ball across the yard. Hershey scampered after it, picked it up, and ran in the opposite direction.

"I'm planning a trip into the woods."

"Why?" His eyes narrowed.

"Have you ever discovered any suspicious fields while scouting the area?"

"Why?"

"Stop asking why. You know why." I lifted my chin. "What if the drug people have fields hidden away and Robert Evans stumbled upon them, thus giving away his identity? It's far-fetched, but it's also plausible."

"The way your mind works is scary." Ann typed into her phone, no doubt letting Davis know of my latest brain scheme. So much for sneaking away.

"You do know how dangerous finding such a field would be, right?" Eric frowned.

"I wouldn't let them see me."

"They would have guards. The place would be well hidden."

"A drone? Danny has one."

"It would be shot down."

"Fine. Bad idea." I pouted. I still think my plan held merit. The more I thought about it, the more my guess changed the location from the mountain to somewhere along the river. Evans was a kayaker. He could have easily pulled on shore and taken a hike. A hike that got him killed.

"Davis said he's already searched the area and found nothing," Ann said, setting her phone on the table. "He also said for you to stop thinking of ways to get in trouble."

"If he had his way, he'd keep me locked in my house until the crook was caught no matter how long it took. By my helping with the investigation, I speed things along."

"By drawing the killer into the open in an attempt to kill you."

"Exactly," Eric said. "We're going to have to be careful and put a lot of thought in how to accomplish this."

"I cannot believe she's convinced you to do this." Ann shook her head.

"The attack at the theater convinced me this has to end. I can't keep losing sleep worrying about my girl."

My heart warmed. "You don't need to worry. Ann is here."

"Ann can't stop a bullet."

"Neither can you." Ann's eyes flashed.

"That's why we need to end this." His face appeared carved from stone. For the second time that day, I sensed the anger and stubbornness in my mild-mannered man. Quite impressive. Especially because it came with his wanting to keep me safe.

"Let's go kayaking again on Eric's next day off. Maybe make a night of it somewhere along the river," I said. "It will all look perfectly normal, but with Eric's knowledge of the area, he might spot something suspicious now that he's looking for it. Mags and Larry can come along. Safety in numbers and all that. I presume his background check came back clean?"

Ann nodded. "He's actually ex-military police. A good man to have around in a time like this. That will give us three out of five people who know how to handle a gun. Please tell me Mags hasn't purchased one."

"Not that I know of." She wouldn't have to worry about me. Since the drive-by shooting that killed my cousin, I refuse to touch the things. "I'd like to buy some pepper spray and a Taser."

"Those are only good close up, CJ. You should also consider taking a self-defense class." Ann stood. "Anyone hungry? I can make soup. It won't hurt CJ's throat."

"That sounds wonderful," I said.

When she continued to stand there staring at me, I realized she wanted me to follow her into the house. With a sigh, I pushed to my feet. Soon after, my house bulged at the seams with three adults and two dogs.

While Ann warmed cans of soup in the

microwave, Eric and I sat on the sofa, legs touching, feet propped on the chest I now used as a coffee table. The dogs, worn out from playing, slept under our stretched legs. Through the window opposite us, Mags and Larry strolled past her house. Ex-military, huh? The more protective hands the better, I guessed.

I couldn't help but feel disappointment that Larry hadn't been the killer. This would all have been over then. Why did I keep getting involved? My gaze fell on the sleeping Caper. Oh, yeah. I inherited a dog with a nose for finding things she shouldn't, which set me on a path of danger to find the bad guy before they did away with me.

My life sure went from boring to anything in a short time. I turned my head as a snore escaped Eric. Poor guy. Losing sleep over me was a sweet gesture but unnecessary. If he kept this up, he'd be a walking zombie soon. Trouble wasn't something I could stay out of. I slowly rose to my feet and joined Ann in the kitchen. "Let's take the soup outside so we don't wake him."

She nodded. "I want to speak with Larry about being extra protection for you. Davis seems to think it necessary." My eyes widened. Did that mean Davis expected the danger to increase shortly? What did the authorities know that I didn't?

Chapter Eleven

I woke the next morning to find Ann gone. I smiled, enjoying the privacy to stretch and groan at my leisure. My joy faded fast when swallowing reminded me of my tortured throat.

I shuffled down the stairs, fixed myself my usual morning cup of coffee, and headed for the front door. The handle turned easily enough, but something blocked the door from the other side.

Caper whined at my feet, her wide, dark eyes on me. When I didn't open the door to let her out, she barked.

Thundering back upstairs, I grabbed my cell phone and called Ann. "Where are you?"

"Talking with Larry."

"I'm locked in my house."

"That's so you can't go anywhere without me." Click.

What? I frowned at the device in my hand. She'd locked me in? I'd throttle her. I called Eric.

"Can you come unblock my door? Ann locked me in."

"Really? I'm sorry, sweetheart, but I'm on the river."

"Okay." I called Roy who promised to be there in less than five minutes.

True to his word, he let me out and pointed to a two-by-four that had kept the door shut. "Most likely a prank." He took the wood and returned to his cart.

When Ann arrived, I sat at my picnic table, coffee in hand, and smiled. "Good morning."

She winced. "I forgot to alert someone to my plan."

"Don't ever lock me in again. I am not your prisoner."

"I didn't want to wake you to have you go with me." She jerked her head toward Mags's house. "When Larry pulled up, I wanted to talk to him before he left."

"And?" I glared over the rim of my cup.

"He's going to help keep an eye on you and agreed to a camping trip down the river." Her eyes sparkled.

"You aren't opposed to my crazy idea of hunting for a field that might not exist, and if it does, increases the danger?"

"It might get me fired." She shrugged. "But on the other hand, it might help solve this case. I've kind of been thinking of going into the private investigator business anyway."

My eyes widened. "I thought you loved being a cop."

"I do, but there are a lot of restrictions. I'd have more freedom if I wasn't." She wiggled her eyebrows. "Then you could hire me to watch your back while you search for trouble."

I laughed. "I doubt I could afford you. Don't think that because you're in agreement with me that I'm not mad at you."

She waved a dismissive hand. "You'll get over it. Eric is scouting out a place to camp. When he returns, we'll pack up and head out to rough it for a day or two. We've been assigned the task of purchasing the food. How soon can you be ready?"

"As soon as I change. Why don't you make a list?" I jumped to my feet and rushed inside to change.

Fifteen minutes later, in Ann's brown Chrysler, we headed for the grocery store. "This is an old-lady car. Doesn't seem to suit you."

"Don't be a car snob. I love this old girl. Used to belong to my mom."

I understood. It's the reason I still had Grams's house. We'd have to clean it out when we returned from camping so Ann could rent it. The income wouldn't hurt my bank account any, and I'd make a friend happy at the same time.

We parked a few spots away from the doors to the store. I grabbed a basket while Ann, who had the list, led the way. "We're picking up the food, but everyone will contribute their share of what it costs. I'm going to make chili for one of the nights."

Ann might have been rambling on about a carefree camping trip, but the way her gaze darted here and there let me know she kept aware of her surroundings. No one paid us undue attention and we moved quickly through the store, filling our basket. Larry was supplying the ice chests, so Ann added four bags of ice to the cart.

"It looks like enough food for a week," I said, peering at the growing pile.

"It's better to be prepared." She tossed in a couple bags of potato chips. "I like to munch when I'm camping." A case of bottled water took up the bottom rack.

The cart grew heavier by the minute. "I guess with five people, we need a lot."

A couple of hundred dollars later, we loaded the purchases into her massive trunk. "You could hide a dead body in there." I cut her a sideways glance.

"Good thing I'm one of the good guys." She closed the trunk and headed for the driver's side, while I climbed in the passenger seat. "With the way your mind works, you should write a book." She put on her seatbelt before turning the key in the ignition.

"I'd rather live the adventure than write about it." I grinned, clicking my seatbelt into place.

"You are doing that." She pulled out of the parking lot and headed for the interstate. After a short distance, she kept glancing in her rearview mirror.

I turned to look out the back window. "What?"

"That truck has been following us since we left the store."

"This is the only interstate."

"My cop sense tells me something's up." She

pressed the accelerator.

Wonderful. I gripped the door handle. “I hope you can outrun them.”

“I took a defensive driving class.” She increased speed again.

I glanced back. The truck loomed larger in the window. “We can’t outrun them in this old car.”

“We can try. Hand me my phone.”

I reached down and grabbed it from the console. “How are you going to drive and hold this?”

“Right. Put it on speaker.”

I did and held it up to her mouth.

“Call Davis.” The phone connected. “This is Lowery. We are being chased by a late model Ford F-150, forest green in color. We’re headed south and just passed mile-marker 108. Requesting backup.”

“On its way,” Davis replied.

The truck rammed us. My head jerked forward. “We’re going to die.”

“We’ve been hit, sir.”

“Keep your wits about you, Lowery.” Click.

She glared at me. “No more talk like that. We are not going to die, but whoever is driving that truck is going to pay if they hurt this car.”

The truck hit us again. The car fishtailed. I prayed the ones paying wouldn’t be us. “You passed our exit.”

“I’m not leading this guy anywhere near the community.” She took the next exit and circled back to the interstate, our pursuer close on our tail.

The next ram from the truck sent us into the

median and out the other side. Horns blared as Ann fought to turn us back the right way. She rocketed back across the median, pulling behind the truck.

"How do you like it, scumbag?" A manic look gleamed in her eyes.

The truck slammed on its brakes.

Ann whipped the steering wheel to the right to keep from plowing into it. Now, we were again in front of the truck.

My breath came in gasps. The hand gripping the door handle turned slick with sweat. I laughed with glee at the sound of approaching sirens.

The truck sped up, taking the next exit. Ann followed. "We can't lose him."

"Backup won't know where to find us." My throat dried up.

She pulled to the side of the road and stopped. "Dang it." She pounded the steering wheel, then shoved her door open and marched to the back of the car.

I followed on trembling legs. The rear bumper barely held on. Both rear lights had shattered from the impact. The trunk smashed. "I bet our eggs are goners."

Ann jerked her attention to me, then burst in laughter. "That's what you're concerned about? You beat all, CJ." She turned as a squad car, Milton at the wheel, parked behind us. "You're too late."

"I did my best," he said, unfolding his large frame from the car. "Are the two of you all right?"

"We're fine." Ann pointed at the car. "She isn't."

"That can be fixed." He took a picture of the

paint smear on the left fender. “Not much to go on. Could you see the driver?”

“Only that the person wore a baseball cap pulled low. Could be male or female.”

“I agree,” I said when he looked my way. “Too hard to tell when I was holding on for dear life.”

“You two head home. I’ll take things from here.” Milton strode back to his car, leaving us standing there like lost hitchhikers.

“Might as well see what damage was done and replace anything broken, eggs or otherwise, at the small store near your house.” Ann pulled on the trunk, finally forcing it to open with a metal screech. “Eggs are fine. Wow.” Other than some crushed chips and dented cans, we were good. No need to stop anywhere else.

I rushed back to my seat and jumped in. “Come on. I don’t want to be here if that truck comes back.”

We sped home and stopped next to my house where Eric, Larry, and Mags waited at the outdoor table. They froze at the sight of Ann’s battered car.

“Sorry we’re late,” I said, motioning toward the trunk. “We had a bit of trouble with a truck intent on running us off the road. All is fine.”

Eric wrapped me in his arms. “Are you sure?”

“Other than my heart racing faster than a twister, yes.” I leaned my head on his broad chest. “Ann is one heck of a driver. Should be a racecar driver with Nascar.”

“I’ll unload the trunk.” Larry pushed to his feet. “You two rest a bit.”

That sounded wonderful. I sat on the bench and

let the men handle the rest.

"You have all the excitement," Mags said. "Seriously."

"You're welcome to that kind of excitement if it's something you crave." I took some deep breaths. "We could have crashed into a tree and died in a fiery car wreck, but okay."

She shook her head. "After that, we're venturing into the wild. Makes you wonder about our mental state, doesn't it?"

I giggled, which quickly turned into a stomach-aching, tears-streaming, totally-lost-my-mind laughing fit. I held a hand to my sore throat but couldn't stop.

Mags tossed the contents of her water glass in my face. "Snap out of it."

My eyes widened. I gasped at the iciness, then started laughing again. Yep, I'd lost my ever-picking mind.

"Something's wrong with this girl," Mags said. "Eric?"

He handed me a towel from the corner of the table. "CJ?"

"I'm…fine." I snorted and wiped my dripping face. "Let me go make sure I have everything I need for Caper while you load up whatever vehicles we're taking." I eyed the colorful kayaks in the back of a red truck, which I presumed belonged to Larry.

Back in the house, I gathered not only my wits, but Caper's food and water dishes, along with her box of food packets. I clipped her leash onto her collar, grabbed my duffel bag, and joined the others outside. Our next step could well be the one that solved the case or resulted in the end of us. “You all sure about this?”

They nodded.

“As long as we stay together, we should be fine.” Ann typed into her phone. “I sent Milton a text that we were headed into the woods for a few days. If we aren’t back in three, he’ll track my phone. Let’s go catch a drug lord.”

Chapter Twelve

Larry dropped us women off on the river's shore, then he and Eric went to drop off the truck at our exit point. While we waited for them to return, Ann paced the area between me and the road, her hand on the butt of her gun as if she were Annie Oakley.

"Stand still," Mags ordered. "You're making me nervous, and I am not a skittish person." She shooed away Hershey, who seemed determined to climb in her lap.

I patted my leg for the dog to come near me and glanced around for Caper. Seeing her leash sticking out from under a bush, I pulled her to my side and put my foot on the end to keep her in place. "The last thing we need is for you to dig up something else."

"Ain't that the truth." Mags heaved a sigh. "We could be halfway down the river in the time it takes to drive to the end and back."

A slight exaggeration. "They'll be here soon."

"We're sitting ducks out here."

Ann turned. "Nobody but Milton knows we're here. You're safe."

"Says the woman with the gun. All we have are Tasers and pepper spray." Mags faced me. "You did bring yours, right?"

I showed her where it hung from the strap of my backpack. "I learn from my mistakes. It's better to be armed."

Ann looked relieved when the men arrived. Before they were out of the truck, she was tossing camping gear onto the rafts we'd pull behind the kayaks.

"I thought you girls would have had this done already?" Eric's brow furrowed.

"Ann wanted us to sit still while she guarded us." I jumped to my feet and placed Caper in the kayak I'd be using. "I've never paddled one of these before."

"It's easy," Eric said. "You'll catch on fast." He tossed me a life jacket. "Keep that close at hand. I'll be paddling right beside you."

I waded into the water and climbed ungracefully into the kayak. It rocked back and forth as if tossed on a stormy sea. I yelped and gripped the sides.

Laughing, Eric climbed into his without mishap and gripped his paddle. "Take yours like this."

I put my hands at a comfortable distance apart. A few feet away, Larry instructed Mags in the art of kayaking. "Why couldn't we have a tandem one?"

"Because of all the stuff we need to drag behind us. Dip your paddle like this, then like this, until you gain a comfortable rhythm."

I mimicked his moves and skimmed across the water. "This is like flying."

"Let the river carry you. You don't want to tire yourself out." Eric caught up with me. "Don't go too far ahead of everyone."

I rested my paddle in my lap and waited on the others, letting the current carry me along. I felt like a cardboard cutout at a shooting range. Anyone with a gun could pick us off one by one from behind the thick foliage on shore.

Obviously, Ann felt the same way because she rode so close our paddles hit. "Sorry."

"Give me some space." I glared.

"Is there a road nearby?" Larry glanced around us. "I thought I heard a vehicle."

"The same one we drove down," Eric said. "It on the other side of those trees, then veers away from the river at the exit point. We're going past there. If anyone is growing anything illegal, it won't be on the beaten path."

"Will it look suspicious passing the exit point?" I flexed my fingers, which had grown sore from gripping the paddle.

"We won't be the first." He scanned one side of the river, then the other. "I'm pretty sure we weren't followed, but keep your eyes open just in case."

I nodded and pulled the brim of my cap down to shade my eyes as I perused each shoreline. For what, I had no idea unless something jumped out at me.

Our approach startled a white-tailed deer and it bounded back into the forest. A squirrel scampered up a tree and chattered down at us. Soon we reached bluffs that rose high above our heads. Stubborn trees and bushes fought for footholds on the rock. We floated on a truly magical place. If I tried hard enough, I could almost pretend we were going on a normal, fun-filled camping trip instead of an excursion into danger.

I wouldn't dwell on that right now. I'd focus on the beauty of the day and the promise of two days with Eric.

Storm clouds gathered overhead and blocked the sun, taking with it some of the day's heat. I pushed my cap back. "We should hurry. We don't want to be out here if it storms. Lightning and water are not friends."

"Agreed." Eric motioned to the others to hurry. "We want to set up camp before the rain starts."

We paddled harder but not fast enough. The clouds dropped their burden as we pulled up to the clearing Eric had chosen. We were soaked before getting out of our kayaks.

Eric started assembling the large tent. For our safety, we'd decided on a communal one rather than two, one for the men and the other for the women. No time for modesty, Ann told us. We'd have to be one big family, snores and all.

Larry secured the kayaks, then erected a smaller tent to hold our supplies. Everything in our backpacks and duffel bags would have to be set out in the sun once it made its appearance. For now, we three women huddled together in wet misery under tree branches that offered little protection. I hoped it wasn't a harbinger of the rest of our camping trip.

"All right, ladies. In the tent." Eric held the flap open. "Change into dry clothes if you can."

We didn't need to be told a second time. Mags, spry for a woman in her mid-fifties, beat Ann and me inside. She held up a plastic bag of clothes. "Mine won't be damp at all."

"Smarty-pants. I used a waterproof duffle bag." I grinned. "Ann?"

"I'll be shivering until a fire is built." She frowned. "How did two city girls think of wrapping their clothes in waterproof bags?"

I shrugged. "It made sense going out on the water."

"You're smarter than you appear." She stripped out of her wet clothes.

"Here." I tossed her a pair of yoga pants several inches too short and the baggy tee-shirt I'd planned on using as pajamas. "You can give them back when your clothes are dry."

"Thanks." She grinned and quickly dressed in the dry clothes.

After changing, I peered out of the tent to see Eric and Larry wearing slickers and sitting in folding chairs as if the rain didn't still fall. I pulled a slicker from my bag, donned it, and then joined them.

"Aren't y'all cold?" I sat in a chair next to Eric.

"Nah." Eric held up a thermos. "Coffee. The rain will stop soon, and we'll dry off fast enough."

Not in this humidity. I glanced at the sky,

blinking against the drops. A patch of blue gave hope the rain would abate in a few minutes. “I guess we won’t be doing much searching this afternoon.”

“No, we don’t want to leave footprints,” Eric said. “Things will dry up enough by morning. It didn’t rain hard enough to soak the ground.”

So we’d wait and try to occupy ourselves until morning. Once the rain stopped, Eric built a fire and Ann warmed up her chili. We removed our slickers, shaking the water from them. Having paid less than a dollar for each of them, we’d get one more day out of them.

Clothes hung on every branch within reach. Sleeping bags lay unzipped on the ground. Caper and Hershey lay on a pile of damp leaves and watched the proceedings with sorrowful eyes. Poor things. I picked up Caper and put her in the tent. Hershey bounded after us.

Rather than join us around the fire, Ann paced the clearing while her chili heated and studied the tree line, the water’s edge, and the sky. What in the world did she think she’d see up there? Crooks flying over in a helicopter?

When Caper let out a yip, Ann had her gun in her hand before I could blink.

“She’s playing with the puppy.” I rolled my eyes. “You need to relax.”

“I can’t relax on the job. Someone could be watching us right now.”

“Lured by the delicious aroma of her chili.” I grinned.

“It’s no joking matter. Instead of relaxing, maybe you need to be more on alert.” She took a second to stir the pot over the fire.

“You’re alert enough for both of us.” I crossed my arms and propped my feet on the rocks rimming the firepit.

“Ladies, if the two of you keep harping on each other, it’s going to be a long couple of days.” Larry scowled. “I know we have a purpose for being here, but camping is a time of relaxation, clearing the mind, and getting closer to nature. Let’s try a bit of silence.”

When did the newest member of our group get so bossy? I huffed and stared at the flames licking the bottom of the chili pot.

“I do love a take-control man.” Mags moved her chair closer to him and rested her head on his shoulder.

Ugh. The day warmed up and humidity hung heavy in the air. Sitting next to the fire lost its appeal and I stood and headed for the tent designated as the bathroom, complete with a five-gallon bucket and plastic seat.

My feet grew heavier with each step. I glanced down to see leaves and twigs stuck to the bottom of my shoes. Had I stepped in gum in the middle of nowhere? I removed one shoe. Nope. I’d melted the rubber soles by propping my feet too close to the fire. From the laughter behind me, the others knew exactly what I’d done.

“If you didn’t bring another pair,” Eric said, “the rubber will harden. Pull out as much of the debris as you can.”

“Think of it this way.” Ann grinned. “You’ll have a very distinct shoe pattern.”

"Hilarious." After taking care of business, I pulled off what didn't belong on my shoes. Then I rejoined the others in the makeshift kitchen. Ann was dishing out bowls of chili and Mags cut up cornbread.

The homey scene convinced me Larry was right. Today could be a peaceful day of no worries and no danger. I'd have to ignore Ann's pacing and scowling. Why couldn't she be more subtle like Eric and Larry? They cast the occasional glance into the forest, but anyone watching wouldn't think they were doing anything more than seeing why a twig snapped or a branch rustled.

A large splash sounded near the water's edge. We all froze.

"Stay here," Eric whispered, jumping to his feet. "Larry?"

"Right behind you."

The two men went into stealth mode while Ann planted herself in front of Mags and me.

Mags stepped to the side. "I can't see with you in the way."

I peered around my bodyguard friend, my heartbeat in my throat. How could anyone have discovered us so soon?

Eric and Larry stayed as much in the shadows as possible. Another splash sounded.

Larry yelped and jumped back. "Snake."

I frowned. "Snakes don't make loud splashes." I knew that much. So who, or what, had?

Chapter Thirteen

Out of the water galloped a very wet, very frightened, chocolate Labrador puppy. Hershey dashed up to Eric and shook herself, spraying both of them with river water.

"Mystery of the splash solved." Eric glanced toward the tent. "I never saw her get past us."

Mags peered in the tent. "That's because the little rascal chewed a hole in the back of the tent. Anyone got any duct tape?"

Ann scowled. "That dog would chew through that, too. Now any creature that wants can wander through that hole while we're sleeping."

"I'll put an ice chest in front of the hole." Eric clipped a leash on the puppy and hooked her to a tree. "Try getting away now."

I narrowed my eyes at the innocent-looking Caper sitting at my feet. "You'd better not be teaching that little girl your tricks." I received a lick on my leg in response to the warning. "Being cute won't keep you from a scolding, young lady."

Larry poked around the bushes with a stick. "I won't be able to sleep with a hole in the tent and snakes roaming around. I'm sleeping in my chair." Not finding any of the slithery creatures, he returned to his chair and settled in, propping his feet on a rock. "Call it guard duty."

I exchanged an amused glance with Eric, then started blowing up air mattresses. We'd brought along the cheap kind used in a swimming pool, in case we had to make a run for it, or so I'd been told. Better to leave things behind that didn't cost a lot. Ann could be thrifty.

It didn't take long for me to get light-headed from lack of oxygen. I swayed on my feet. Eric took me by the shoulders and set me in a chair. "We don't need you falling into the fire." He picked up a mattress and started to blow.

By the time the sun had fallen behind the mountains, beds were dry and set in place. Larry wrapped his sleeping bag around his shoulders, still refusing to sleep on the ground.

"It's not even fully dark." Mags scowled, standing at the tent entrance.

"We want to get a start at daybreak," Eric said. "Try to sleep anyway. Put something over your eyes."

"You, young man, are too bossy for your britches." She wagged a finger at him, then plopped onto her mattress. She lay on her back, hands folded over her chest like a corpse in a coffin.

I chuckled and spread out on my own makeshift bed. Sleep came slowly. My eyes opened at every snap of a twig, croak of a frog, or buzz of an insect. Name any forest creature, and it kept me awake until far into the night. It felt as if I'd just fallen asleep when Eric called to rise and shine.

Groaning, I pushed to my hands and knees, then to my feet, every bone and muscle in my body protesting. Poor Mags. If I felt like this, how must she feel? I glanced at her mattress to find it empty.

"Come on." She poked her head through the tent opening. "Eric is raring to go. If you want to eat, you'd better do it now."

"Just shoot me and put me out of my misery."

"Poor baby." She rolled her eyes and let the flap fall into place.

I used a baby wipe to wash the sleep from my eyes in a futile attempt to wake up. When I'd finished, I stumbled outside and made a beeline for the pan of hot water on the fire. Bless Eric. He'd already put grounds into a cup for me and started pouring the moment I exited the tent.

"Do you need to borrow a comb?" He patted my head. "You look like a porcupine."

"I feel like I've been run over by a buffalo." I sniffed the java. "I'll be better as soon as this is cool enough to drink."

"You have fifteen minutes."

Not nearly enough time. I lowered into a chair and glanced around for Caper. "Are we taking the animals?"

"It's either that or let a bear get them."

I shuddered. "Okay. Caper is a good warning system, and Hershey's romping will scare away the critters."

"Anyone hear that?" Larry peered at the sky.

I listened, finally hearing a faint buzz. "What is it?"

"Get out of sight." Eric doused the fire with water from the pot, quickly kicked dirt over it, and dragged me into the trees.

A few minutes later, a drone passed, hovering for a few seconds over the campsite. "The tent."

"They won't know whose it is. People camp along this river all the time. Try and see which way the drone goes."

"It's following the river the way we were headed."

He nodded. "That's the way we'll keep going." Once the drone had left, he gathered us in the clearing. "It's no longer a secret there are campers around. I'm not familiar with drones, so don't know how far their range is, but that one looked expensive. I don't think the operator is very close by. We might have a hike ahead of us. Pack plenty of food and water." Eric grabbed his backpack.

We followed his example. When finished we lined up behind him, Ann next, then me, then Mags, and Larry taking up the rear. Eric kept a firm grip on Hershey's leash while I did the same with Caper. The last thing we needed was for the dogs to run ahead and give us away.

The heat and humidity rose with the sun, reminding us we were in the midst of summer in the South. It didn't matter that we were in the mountains. If we stepped into the sun, we melted.

I wiped the back of my hand across my perspiring forehead to keep it from dripping into my eyes. I loved the outdoors, really, but traipsing through a thick forest knowing only danger lay ahead if we were discovered took the joy out of our hike.

What, exactly, did we plan to do if we did discover anything? We couldn't confront them. Did it take all of us to find out information to relay back to Davis? Not for the first time, I reconsidered the decision to go on the hunt.

Of course, knowing who we were up against might be a good thing. I doubted we'd recognize anyone if we did see them. I didn't believe they'd be right under our noses or be up to something illegal such as drugs. But then again, it wouldn't be the first time. I'd been fooled before by a friendly face.

Eric held up his hand to stop us. "Five-minute break."

Thank you, God. I dropped my back and sat on it. From the side pouch, I pulled a bottle of water and drank half before putting it back.

"I officially hate hiking." Mags plopped next to me. "I should have stayed home with my cat."

"Why haven't you given her a name?" I'd always wondered.

"She wouldn't come when called if I did, so why bother?"

"It's the right thing to do."

"Why are we talking about this when there are more important things afoot, like finding a drug dealer?" Her eyes widened. "If it's so important to you, then you name her."

"Fine. I'm going to call her Calico." I stood

and put my pack on my back and resumed my place in line.

"No more talking," Ann said. She pointed overhead to where a drone zipped past.

Thankfully, we were under heavy tree coverage. Whoever owned the drone took their secrecy very seriously. Maybe I should have let Ann lock me in my house and let the authorities hunt these people down.

But what if the bad guys came for me while my friends were gone? What if they killed my friends while I stayed safely behind a locked door? My worries zipped from one corner of my mind to the other. I wasn't a coward. Never had been, but I might be a fool for not walking away from that first mystery. I felt like a junkie looking for the next fix no matter the cost.

Eric glanced back at me, concern on his face. He always knew when I was troubled. He raised a brow. I gave him the okay signal.

Caper stopped and gave a low woof, causing everyone to duck and freeze. When nothing seemed to be where she looked, Eric waved us on. I glanced back and smiled as a squirrel scampered up a tree. "Good girl," I whispered. What a wonderful warning system a dog was. We might not be in mortal danger from a squirrel, but Caper noticed something we hadn't.

Mags stumbled behind us, drawing Eric's attention. I glanced back to see Larry put his arm around her waist and help her steady herself. I was glad to be wrong about him. Mags did need someone to love her and erase the loneliness that sometimes drifted off her like waves.

Eric called a lunch break, saying we had thirty minutes. He sat next to me and handed me a piece of jerky and a package of cheese and crackers. "It isn't much," he said, softly, "but it will give you fuel."

"Thanks." I bit into the jerky. "I'm having second thoughts about all of this." We kept our voices low.

"I'm not."

"Why?" I gave him a questioning look.

"I want this to be over. I want to know who we're dealing with so we can better alert the authorities and keep everyone safe."

"We might die today."

"We might." He gave a sad smile. "There was no turning back once that note was placed on the windshield of your car. Going on the defense is our best plan of action."

Ann moved next to us. "I'm with Eric." She pulled her cell phone from her pocket. "I've been placed on probation. Guess I'll be starting my private investigation business soon."

"I'm sorry." I put a hand on her arm. "You told us we shouldn't do this."

"I made the choice to come along." She shrugged. "It's the silver lining in a stormy cloud."

I nodded. She had mentioned wanting to go out on her own for more freedom. "Well, I'm sure there will be a reason for me to hire you in the future. I'm like a magnet for people wanting to commit murder."

She snorted back a laugh. "Thank you for

brightening my day."

"You're welcome." I hoped Davis wouldn't arrest us when we returned. If we returned.

We walked another fifteen minutes before Eric stepped into a clearing, then jumped back as if on fire, knocking me to the ground. He motioned for us all to stay low and mouthed, "Sorry."

On my hands and knees, I crawled to peer through the brush. A field of pretty red flowers stretched in front of us. Off to the side marijuana plants grew tall, reaching for the sun. Patrolling the fields were two men on four-wheelers.

Caper barked.

Chapter Fourteen

I froze in mid-crouch. The four-wheelers roared around the field. It soon became apparent they hadn't heard my naughty dog. I scooped her into my arms, put my hand around her snout, and sprinted in the opposite direction.

Multiple feet pounded behind me. I stopped to catch my breath when I could no longer hear the four-wheelers.

Mags put a hand on her chest and sagged against Larry. "Mercy. What a rush."

I blinked a few times before realizing she actually had fun running from two men guarding illegal fields. "You're crazy."

"I don't think they saw us," Ann said. "Tell me someone had the presence of mind to put the coordinates into their phone."

"I did." Larry held up his device. "I also suggest we get going. Mags stepped in the mud back there. It won't be hard to tell someone watched from the trees."

I didn't need to be told twice. Reciting the coordinates I'd seen over and over in my mind, and with my heart still in my throat, I set off for camp. Eric soon took the lead. Funny how fear can make even tired feet move faster.

With limbs that trembled from fatigue, I helped dismantle camp and secure everything back on the rafts. The sun was setting when we pulled away from shore. Tree shadows stretched across the river, lending the evening a haunted look.

Paddling against the current was a lot harder than going with it. Trying not to make any more noise than necessary, I paddled slow, long strokes, and pushed past the pain in my arms and shoulders. Thankfully, the exit point was a lot closer than where we'd put in. Not wanting to leave us without protection, Eric and Mags elected to drive and fetch the other vehicle.

Eric cupped my face in his hands and leaned his forehead against mine. "Don't be foolish, sweetheart. If danger comes, run. I'll find you."

I nodded, my throat clogging with emotion. I raised my face for a kiss and watched through tears as he climbed into the driver's seat of the truck. Ann and Larry stood close by my side.

"I'm not the only one needing protection now." I started unloading the kayaks. "You were there. If they find out it was us, we'll all have targets on our back."

"Thanks for the reminder." Ann hefted an ice chest from the raft.

"You keep a lookout," Larry said. "CJ and I

can handle this."

"We'll get done faster with all three. I want to get out of here as soon as the others return." Ann reached for a sleeping bag.

The supplies were piled and the kayaks pulled on shore before the other two returned. "Shouldn't they be back by now?" I stood in the middle of the road looking for headlights.

"Yes." Larry pushed the button on his watch to illuminate the face.

The moon rose higher in the sky. Cotton filled my mouth. Where were they? Had the drug people found them? Were they lying dead in a ditch? Held captive?

My breathing quickened. "I'm going to start walking."

Ann grabbed my arm. "We don't know what we'd be headed into."

"Staying here doesn't sound any better." I pulled my arm free and headed up the road.

The other two followed. We walked in silence, stopping at every snap of a twig or rustle of brush. My nerves stretched tighter than my jeans after Thanksgiving dinner.

Larry put a hand on both mine and Ann's shoulders. "Shh. Hear that?"

The rumble of a car engine. I peered through the moonlit night. "I don't see anything."

"Let's get off the road."

We'd no sooner moved out of sight than Eric's jeep sped by without its headlights on. We jumped into the road and waved our arms.

Brake lights blazed red.

We dashed for the vehicle, yanking doors open.

"Where's the other car?" I leaned over the front seat. "Why do you have your jeep instead of the truck?"

Eric rocketed us forward. "We had to leave the other vehicle. I drove off a ways to turn around before Mags transferred to the truck, but when we reached it, men surrounded it, their guns at the ready. We waited for them to leave, but when they didn't, we came back to get you."

"I love that truck," Larry said.

"What about the stuff?"

"Not worth our lives."

"Is there another way out of here?"

He nodded. "Pray it isn't blocked. We won't win a gunfight with those guys."

My blood ran cold. What would we do if the road was blocked? We couldn't very well run over whoever stood in our way.

Mags tossed her muddy shoes out the window. "So they can't match the footprint to me."

The absurdity sent me into a fit of giggles. I wrapped my arms around my waist to contain the laughter. It didn't work.

Mags stared over her shoulder. "The stress is too much. She's lost her mind."

"Do…you…still think…this is…fun?" I asked.

"We're living an adventure movie. I have complete faith in Eric to get us out of here." She turned back around.

Eric glanced at me in the rearview mirror. From the crease in his brow, he didn't have the same faith in himself Mags did.

I caught my breath and regained my composure. "Sorry. The shoes out the window struck me funny."

"You'll regret tossing them if we end up having to walk out of these woods," the always-practical Ann said.

We drove a while in silence. My eyelids drooped as the adrenaline wore off, only to snap fully open when the jeep slowed.

"We're coming up on the intersection. Everyone get down. If anyone is there, I'm hoping my ranger jeep will have them thinking I'm on patrol."

We ducked. I wrapped my arms around my knees and prayed as I might in a plane making an emergency landing.

Eric flipped on his headlights and increased his speed. He waved at someone on the side of the road and continued without slowing. "We're good. There were two men, but I didn't see any guns, and they didn't flag me down."

"That could mean they now have someone suspicious to watch," Ann said. "Other than Larry's truck, that is. If they know how, they can trace it back to him. Then we're all screwed."

"Thanks for the positivity." Mags crossed her arms. "We got out of the woods. Let's meet one challenge at a time, okay?"

"The challenges are getting harder," I mumbled. "Like a reality show gone wrong."

"And the only prize is your life." Eric smiled in the mirror. "I agree with Mags. One thing at a time, please."

"I'll report the truck stolen," Larry said. "That ought to keep me from getting killed in a drive-by shooting."

"Good idea. I'll text Milton." Ann punched keys on her cellphone. "I hate lying to him, but at this point in time, I don't see an alternative. You'll have to go to the station and fill out a report. When it's discovered you filed falsely, you could be arrested."

"Won't be the first time." He laughed. "I won't be job hunting or anything where I need to worry about a list of arrests."

Seriously, who was this man?

"Wait a minute. Is there anything tying any of us to the camping equipment we left?" I stiffened. "We rented those kayaks."

"Under my name," Larry said. "Guess I might not be out of that woods after all, but I could say those things were in the back of my truck when it was stolen."

I hoped it would work. It had to.

Eric dropped Larry at his house, then drove to Heavenly Acres to drop off Mags. "I'm spending the night on CJ's sofa."

I doubted any of us would sleep well that night.

Chapter Fifteen

Other than make my rounds each morning, I stuck close to the house for the next few days, worrying every time Eric set out into the woods to do his job. It didn't take long for cabin fever to set in. Especially with a cop on probation who paced the floor, the yard, wherever we were at the moment.

"Why don't you occupy yourself setting up your PI business?" I glared when she passed the picnic table for the umpteenth time. "Or are you having second thoughts?"

"Second thoughts." She sighed and sat across from me. "Probation isn't the same as being fired. Now that losing my job is a real possibility, I find myself uncertain. I have a job. Going into business for myself isn't a sure thing for making a living." Her face brightened. "Why don't we go clean out your grandmother's house? It would give us something to do and get me closer to moving in when this is over."

"Great idea." I hopped up and ran into the house for my purse. I might not be emotionally ready to remove Grams's things, but I also didn't want to wait around for a killer to show up. No one would know to look for me there.

Purse in hand, I opened the front door and smashed my nose against Ann's back. "Why are you standing in front of the door?" I rubbed my nose.

"I'm guarding you. It's my job."

"Is it?" I squeezed past her. "You're on probation, so technically, you shouldn't be working."

She spun, eyes wide. "You want me to stop guarding you? We're friends. I care what happens to you." She shook her head. "No, I can't stop watching you until this is all over."

Knowing she wouldn't abandon me filled me with a small sense of safety, but that was my secret. I climbed into the driver's seat of my Prius and within twenty minutes parked in the driveway of the house I'd lived in for five years before moving to Heavenly Acres.

I sat and stared through the windshield. Someone had mowed the yard. Most likely Eric, the sweetheart. Once Ann moved in, she'd keep things up. I stepped onto the driveway.

"You alright?" Ann peered at me over the roof of the car.

"I'm fine. This is long overdue." I unloaded some boxes from the backseat of the car, then climbed the front porch steps and opened the door.

"Welcome to your new home—soon, I hope." I waved Ann in. "Let's pile all boxes, papers, photo albums and anything else that looks personal in the middle of the kitchen table, and we'll sort through them."

While Ann moved to a bookcase, I headed for Grams's bedroom. My heart caught at the handstitched quilt on the bed and the frilly white curtains on the window. How could I let someone else sleep in her room? I folded the quilt. It would look wonderful on my bed, and I could sleep each night wrapped in something Grams had made.

I dropped old perfume bottles into a garbage can and packed her jewelry box in the container on her dresser. I'd sort through it later. Her clothes I'd donate to a charity, so I emptied drawers into boxes before moving to her closet.

Carrying armloads of clothes she hadn't worn in over ten years, I lay them across her bed. People who appreciated vintage would love some of these. I smiled at a suit that looked as if it could have graced the cover of a women's magazine in the fifties. Grams hated to get rid of anything, saying clothes eventually came back in style.

Once I'd removed all the hanging clothes, I took down box after box from the top shelf. Maybe I would need more than one day to sort through them all. I started carrying the boxes to the kitchen table.

"Any receipts can be thrown out unless it looks important," I said. "I'll sort through the rest."

Ann nodded. "I've put the photo albums on that end of the table. I thought you'd like to look through them at your leisure."

"Thank you." I smiled and returned to Grams's room to check under the bed. Reaching under, I pulled out an old battered suitcase. Opening it, I discovered letters bound with red ribbon. My hand went to my heart. She'd kept the letters from my grandfather. How romantic. Before carrying the suitcase out, I took one last look around Grams's room. Maybe someday it would be mine, but that wasn't in the near future.

I sighed and moved down the hall to the bedroom where I'd lived the last few years. Since Grams had decorated it in pink and yellow when I was young, it remained the same. I'd removed posters of teenage heartthrobs a while back, but the outdated bedspread made me wince.

I wandered around the room, clearing off the dresser of childish things. After Grams's death, I took everything of importance with me. With the drawers and closet emptied, the next stop was the bathroom.

By lunchtime, the one-bath, two-bedroom house's contents were boxed up, bagged up, or waited on the dining room table to be sorted through. "Want to order a pizza?" I opened the refrigerator. Nothing. The freezer revealed three full trays of ice. Thank you, God. "And something to drink?"

"Sure." Ann pulled out her phone and ordered a large pepperoni pizza and a liter of diet cola.

I opened the first box and sorted through warranties while we waited for the pizza. Every appliance warranty had expired. The entire box was garbage. The next box held faded receipts, some almost twenty years old. Who kept these things? Grams, that's who. By the time the pizza arrived, the garbage overflowed, and boxes to be tossed were stacked up next to it.

"She believed in saving everything," Ann said, frowning at a receipt no longer legible.

"Yep." I pulled another box toward me, then changed my mind. I'd rather stroll down memory lane in a photo album.

Yellowed photos of my mother as a child filled the pages. Some had my grandmother, but most of them were photos of my mother alone. I'd never realized it before, but there were none of my grandfather. I glanced around the living room. All personal belongings had been stowed in boxes, but I couldn't remember seeing a photo of Grandpa.

I chewed the inside of my lip and kept flipping pages, stopping at one of my mother dressed for the prom with my father beside her. "I never realized how much I look like her." I turned the album so Ann could see.

"Wow." A piece of sauce dripped from the slice of pizza in her hand. "Twins."

"Hey. These are priceless." I wiped the spot off the plastic sleeve. "How would you like it if I dropped food on your badge?"

She grinned. "Sorry. Here, have a drink." She handed me a glass of diet soda. "Thanks for leaving all the dishes and linens. What I have isn't much."

"No problem, although they'll probably need washing." I turned my attention to the next photo album. I'd need to find a creative way to store them in my tiny house. Maybe at the bottom of one of the new chests I'd found at the flea market. Surely, I could find room for—I counted ten thick albums. Maybe it would be best to put them in the hollow space under my floorboards.

I bit into my lunch and pulled another album close to me. Oh, these were black and white ones of Grams. I also resembled her. Genes ran strong in the women of our family. Except, Grams had been a bit more rounded in spots and could have been a pinup model.

I chuckled at some of her fooling around with friends in a lake, dangling her legs off the back of a pickup, lying on a blanket in the grass, always surrounded by both girls and boys, but one boy in particular watched her from afar. A secretive smile graced his lips.

Leaning over the photo, I tried to remember where I'd seen him before. I shrugged and turned the page to see the boy kissing Grams on the cheek. Joy sparkled from her eyes. Another photo showed them kissing.

I sat back. Could this be my grandfather?

Shoving the rest of my slice of pizza into my mouth, I opened the suitcase and pulled out the letters. Rather than read the entire page of flowery words, I focused on the Dear, Lovely, Sweet, Annie—my grandmother. Every letter was signed by a man named Larry.

My heart rate increased. "Ann, look at this and tell me who you think it is." I turned the album around and tapped my finger on the boy's face.

She narrowed her eyes, then gasped. "That's

Larry Acres."

I nodded. "He's chummy with my grandmother."

"That doesn't make any sense. He's dating Mags. This man would be too old."

Right. I rubbed my tired eyes. "Could he be Larry's father?"

She shrugged. "Maybe. Read these letters and see what you can find out."

Reading the love letters seemed so personal, but curiosity got the better of me. I read page after page of how much Larry loved my grandmother, how badly he wanted to marry her, but duty for his country called. Then, I read of how much their one night of love had meant to him before he shipped off. There were no more letters, but a telegram inside an envelope informed Grams that Larry had died doing his duty.

Could Larry Acres be her illegitimate son? If so, that would make him my uncle. Mother had never mentioned a brother.

Is that why Larry started coming around? Did he know about Grams? What if he only paid attention to Mags to get closer to me?

My mind spun faster than I could keep up. I rested my head in my hands.

When I'd asked questions as a child about my grandfather, Grams always answered with a smile gracing her lips. She'd told me he died in the army. The pieces fell into place.

"I need to have a conversation with Larry."

Chapter Sixteen

"Yes, Larry seems to have kept a secret from you, but that doesn't mean he's a crook." Eric handed the photo and letter back to me.

"It's suspicious." I glared at his car parked in front of Mags's house.

"Let it be. If he wants to come clean, he will." Eric planted a tender kiss on my cheek. "What are your plans for today?"

"Same as every other day. Make the rounds and try to stay alive." If I didn't die of boredom.

He chuckled. "I like that plan. I'll see you at supper."

I nodded and turned as Ann stepped off the porch. "Ready?"

"Yep." She climbed into the golf cart. "Let's begin another exciting day."

"At least the house is ready for you to move into." I drove us past Mags's house and around the circle.

Luke, son of Norma Waters who resided in number ten, flagged us down. His smile looked forced, although I thought he meant to be friendly and welcoming. “My brother and I want to go out on the river, camp a few nights, that kind of thing. Since you live here, we thought you might know of a good place to pull out and set up camp.”

I bit my lip. In all honesty, I couldn’t direct anyone to where we’d camped. Not only had we left our belongings at the exit spot, but I hadn’t paid close enough attention to details. “I’m sorry. That’s a question best asked of the park ranger. I’ve only been out a few times and didn’t pay much attention other than to marvel at the beauty of the land.”

His smile didn’t fade, but a hard glint came to his eyes. “My mother is the same. No attention to detail. Thanks anyway.” He stomped into the house.

“I’m starting to think her sons live with her.” I glanced at Ann. “Not that I care if they’re crowded or not, but their names should be on the lease. And what kind of man wants to live in a pink and white house?”

“You have worse things to worry about.” She pointed to a tree above us.

I glanced up to see the youngest Olson child, tears streaming down his face, hugging a tree branch. “Are you stuck, Teddy?”

He nodded. “I want down.”

“How long have you been up there?” I parked the cart under the tree in case he fell. It wouldn’t be a soft landing, but it might be better than the ground. “Did you call for help?”

He shook his head. “I didn’t want those mean

men to know I was here."

"What mean men?" Ann asked.

"The ones who live in that house." He pointed to number ten.

"Hold on, buddy. I'm calling your dad to bring a ladder." I called Roy, explained the situation, and then settled in to wait. It didn't take long.

Roy came to an abrupt halt next to us and pulled a folding ladder from the back of his cart. "How many times have I told you not to climb trees unless you can get yourself down?" He leaned the ladder against the tree trunk and climbed up. Once his son was in the cart, Roy climbed in next to him.

"Hold on a moment, Mr. Olson." Ann slid from my cart. "I'd like to ask your son something." She bent over to come face-to-face with Teddy. "Why do you say that man is mean?"

"Because I heard him yelling at his mommy. No one yells at their mommy."

"Did you hear what he said?"

"He said her plan was stupid and wasn't working. That because of it they would all be in trouble."

"Thank you. You've been a big help." She returned to the cart. "I guess I need to speak with the men about a complaint."

"There hasn't been a complaint made." I glanced over to see Mark watching from the window. Uh-oh. His crossed arms and intense stare showed his irritation. "Maybe you should overlook the fact there's been no formal complaint."

"I agree. Stay in the cart." Cop face in place, Ann strolled to the front porch as if she were on a neighborly visit.

I drove away from the tree and stopped in front of the walkway because I couldn't hear from across the road.

Both men stepped outside, the tiny porch barely big enough to hold them both. "Ma'am," they said in unison.

"We've had a complaint of yelling and threats made. Would you know anything about that?" Ann tilted her head.

"Haven't heard a thing," Luke said, then glanced at Mark. "How about you?"

"Not a thing."

"Strange," Ann said, "since the commotion came from here."

"Whoever filed the complaint must have heard the TV," Luke said, shaking his head. "Our mother tends to turn it up loud so she can hear it anywhere in the house."

"Because the house is so large?"

"Yes, ma'am," he said.

"Try to keep it down, please. This is a peaceful community." Ann marched back to me. "Drive on."

"They were lying."

She scowled. "Of course, they were, but without evidence of abuse, we can't do anything. I'll have to catch Norma alone and question her away from her sons."

I agreed, but we had more important things to worry about, not that a woman who might be abused wasn't important. But someone knew someone had located their poppy and pot fields. Soon they'd figure out we were that someone.

Then again, maybe not. I was holding onto the *maybe not* with both hands. I hadn't received any more threats or been followed by suspicious vehicles. All good things.

"What are you grinning about?" Ann leaned over and stared into my face.

"No one has threatened me lately."

"They're biding their time." She propped her feet on the dashboard. "Mark my words. Those guys are as bad as they come. They want you to let your guard down, then they'll pounce."

"Gee, thanks for bringing back the stress." I stopped the cart at the end of the trail to the chapel. I hadn't checked the place in a few days. Now was as good a time as any. I needed the peace the place brought to my heart.

Ann and I walked in silence through a forest, listening to the wind's whispers and the and the birds' songs. A person could almost believe evil didn't exist in the world. Nature had a strong healing power better than any modern medicine.

I reached for the door handle of the chapel and froze, my hand suspended in mid-air. Inside, Danny and Rose were making out hot and heavy for a couple of teenagers. I shot Ann an annoyed look and yanked the door open. "Hey."

They pulled apart as if stung by bees.

"This. Is. A. Church." I planted my fists on my hips. "Can't you do that in the woods somewhere?"

"It's cooler in here." Danny gave a sheepish grin. "Besides, Mags and Larry are in here a lot."

"Making out?" I narrowed my eyes. It appeared I would need to speak with both of them.

He shrugged. "I don't stick around to find out. Gross." He held out his hand to Rose. "Come on."

Keeping her head down, Rose put her hand in his and rose to her feet. "Sorry," she mumbled on her way past us. "Larry and Mags aren't the only ones hanging out in here."

"Hold on." I put a hand on her shoulder. "Explain, please."

"Well, Mom and Dave have been caught trying to find time alone. Then you have those people in number ten. It's hard to hear what people say on the other side of these glass walls, but they always seem to be going at it hot and heavy."

I did not like the picture that portrayed. "Mother and son making out?"

"No, that's disgusting." She made a gagging sound by sticking her finger in her mouth. "Arguing." She gave me a look only teenage girls have mastered and left the chapel with Danny.

"That's two people who have seen Norma and her sons arguing." Ann pressed her lips together. "I need to do some digging into their backgrounds."

"Check and see if they have any connection to Robert Evans." I sat in the front pew. Someday, maybe a pastor would move into Heavenly Acres and people would treat this lovely place more like a church. "There's no television in here they can use as an excuse."

Ann sat next to me and spread her arms along the back of the bench. "It would be too easy for them to be the ones we're looking for."

"Yes, but how better to keep an eye on me than to move in?" I glanced at the glass walls I'd so lovingly restored and felt much like a fish in a bowl. Anyone could take a shot at me and I'd be dead before I knew it. "We'd better leave this place. It's too exposed."

Ann's gaze scanned the trees outside. "Yep."

The hair on my arms rose. I slowly turned, scanning each side of the chapel, trying to see into the forest. "I feel as if someone is watching us."

"Me too."

We quick-walked back to the cart and returned home where Ann took a seat at her laptop to do background checks.

Preferring the old-fashioned way of taking notes, I pulled out a pad of paper and a pencil to add to what I'd previously written. I didn't have a lot to add to possible drug lords, witness protection, and a note left on my car. Volatile people weren't always crooks, but I wrote down Norma and her sons. I added poppy and pot fields. I should have remembered the coordinates Larry had in his phone and jotted them down. I always thought it best to keep all pertinent information in one place even if multiple people had that information.

"Norma Waters is a retired schoolteacher," Ann said. "Mother of two sons, husband deceased. I don't see anything in her background to make me think she's involved."

"The land where the fields are planted is parkland. It's against the law for anyone to plant there."

"Yes, and I'm sure Davis is putting together a plan to make some arrests. It might get rid of the guards and the fields, but what we need to find out is who's at the top."

"How?"

"I don't know." She sighed and closed her laptop. "There's only so much information I can find while on probation. Milton has been ordered not to help me."

We were on our own. "We won't know of any progress they're making." My eyes widened. "We're completely in the dark. This could go on for months, years even."

"Don't overreact. Davis knows what he's doing."

"He's too slow. I want my life back." I crossed my arms and pouted. If I knew what the next step should be, I'd take it. As it was, all I had on my agenda was to talk to Mags and Larry about hanging out in the chapel and Larry's true identity as my uncle.

I had a bit of time before Eric was due to arrive for supper. "I'm going over to Mags's."

"All right." Ann climbed to her feet.

I turned the door handle, which turned, but the door didn't open. Ann wasn't up to her tricks considering she stood behind me. "I think the wood is swollen from the humidity."

"No, we've been locked in." She pointed.

Caper barked.

Smoke drifted under the door.

Chapter Seventeen

Someone tried to burn down my home! I whirled around to meet Ann's worried gaze.

"Out the window." Ann shoved open the nearest one and tossed Caper out. "Now, you."

"I need to get some things." I thundered up the stairs and grabbed important papers and my laptop.

"Now, CJ." Ann shoved a towel under the door.

"The photo albums." I tossed out what I had already gathered, then opened the chest and tossed out priceless albums.

Footsteps pounded on the front porch. A loud whooshing sound followed, then banging.

"CJ. Ann," Larry shouted through the door. "Unlock the door but not with your bare hands. The fire's out."

Ann used the same towel she'd blocked the smoke with to turn the knob. Once the door was open, we stared at Larry who held a fire extinguisher, then down at a pile of smoldering leaves and a burned spot the size of a turkey platter on my front porch.

"Someone is warning you to stay away." Larry shook his head. "I stepped out of Mags's place to head home when I saw the smoke."

"Thank you." I forced a smile. Obviously, the fire hadn't been intended to kill me, although it could have if we'd been asleep and no one noticed the flames. I stepped off the porch and hurried around the corner. "Maybe whoever set the fire got interrupted, or—" I glared at Larry.

"Look, young lady. You've been giving me suspicious looks since I arrived on the scene. I'm not the one behind this. I don't intend you any harm." He exhaled loudly. "We need to have a talk."

I crossed my arms. "Yes, we do. Why don't you go fetch Mags while I clean this up and call Davis?"

"I've already called him." Ann had swept the leaves off the porch and now hauled the water hose to where they stood. "You should save the conversation until after he leaves. I'll order Chinese for supper."

"Fine." I gathered the things I'd tossed out the window and returned them to their proper places. It wasn't until then that I realized Caper was nowhere to be seen. That dog.

"Caper." I stepped back outside. "Come, girl."

"She's under the house." Larry pointed. "Scooted under the minute she was thrown out."

"Poor baby." I knelt down and crooned until

she emerged. Scooping her into my arms, I stood. My gaze fell on a perfect footprint in my flower bed. I glanced at Larry. He wore sneakers. The print belonged to sneakers. "Larry, may I see your foot?"

He glowered. "Why?"

"Just do it and let me know what size shoe you wear."

He growled and came to my side. "That foot is a lot bigger than mine, but it is the same pattern." He held up his foot, showing me the rounded indentations. "Find out who wears a size twelve shoe with that pattern, and you might just find your arsonist." He grinned. "Sorry to disappoint you, but I'm not your bad guy."

I wrinkled my nose. Too bad. I carried my trembling pup into the house and gave her a bacon-flavored treat before taking a seat at the picnic table outside to wait for Davis. When the adrenaline wore off, I started to tremble so violently my teeth chattered. The scorched mark on my porch brought unwelcome tears.

"Oh, sweetie." Mags came up behind me and wrapped her arms around me. "Larry, fetch a blanket. Ann, find some…liquor."

"Gag, no." I hiccupped a laugh. "Can't stand the stuff."

"Then just the blanket and some water." Mags sat next to me and took my hands in hers. Moments later Davis came to an abrupt halt next to the house.

He exited the squad car and headed toward us. "I'll be with you in a minute, CJ. Ann, come with me." He motioned his head for her to follow him.

"You might as well look at the footprint while

you're over there," I called as Larry placed an army blanket around my shoulders. After a few minutes, the heat of the wool blanket had me laying it across the table. "I'm fine. Just a slight breakdown."

"Understandable." Mags patted my back. "You could have burned to death. Horrible way to go, I've heard. Imagine how much it hurts when you burn your finger, then multiply that by a thousand."

"You aren't helping." I laid my head on my crossed arms.

"Sorry. Sit up, Davis is coming."

I jerked upright. From the stony look on his face and the resigned one on Ann's, I gathered their conversation didn't go well.

Ann stopped a few feet away. Davis asked Larry and Mags to join her, then sat across from me.

"You okay?"

"Just shook up."

"Lowery said you've had some misgivings about Larry Acres. Mind explaining those to me? He has an upstanding military record."

"So I've heard." I took a deep breath. "He showed up right when all this started happening. He's keeping important secrets from me. Then, he just happens to be close by when someone sets fire to my house and conveniently puts it out before I'm killed. Coincidence?"

"There's no way that's his footprint on the side of the house. What about the residents in number ten?"

"The sons might have feet that size. Are you going to question them?"

"I don't have any grounds to question them.

What kind of secret is Acres keeping?"

"It's personal in regard to my family. If he's innocent, it doesn't pertain to this case." I crossed my arms.

"I'd bet my badge he's innocent, CJ." Davis rolled his head. "You increase my stress."

"Sorry."

"Tell me more about number ten."

I shrugged. "Norma seems clean. Her sons have no softness. She paid her deposit. The only thing is they've been heard fighting on more than one occasion." I explained what I knew. "They claim Norma is hard of hearing and it's the television the children heard."

Davis jotted down all I'd told him, then pushed to his feet as the Chinese delivery man arrived. Davis declined my invitation to stay and eat. "I'm heading over to Amber's. You were my last task for the day. Good. Eric is here. Be careful, CJ."

Eric glanced at Davis who climbed in the squad car, then at my porch, then at me, worry creasing his brow. "What did I miss this time?" He sat next to me and put his arm around me.

I explained the arson, the footprint, and that I needed to have a serious conversation with Larry. "We'll talk over supper. I'm starved."

Once the others filled their plates from the assorted boxes of food in front of us, I began. "First, I'd like to ask Mags and Larry not to use the chapel as a dating place. It's a church."

Mags frowned. "Who said we do that? We go there for the peace and quiet and to talk."

"There's something special about that chapel in

the woods," Larry said. "We'd never desecrate it."

Unlike a couple of teenagers. "All right, someone misunderstood." I dipped a spring roll into sauce, stalling so I could collect my thoughts. I didn't want to come across as combative. "The next thing is…well, Ann and I visited Grams's house to clean out personal things and came across several photographs." I met Larry's resigned gaze. "Hello, uncle."

"What?" Mags and Eric said in unison.

"It's true, isn't it, Larry? Your father and my grandmother. But you aren't the son of my grandfather."

"It's true." His words were clipped. "My father and your grandmother had a thing before he went away to war. From what my grandmother told me, they intended to get married, but he didn't come back." Sorrow replaced sarcasm. "Your grandmother had no means of supporting herself, much less a child, so my father's parents raised me. It wasn't until they passed and I went through some letters sent to me by my birth mother that I learned the truth.

"Your mother is my half-sister."

"Yet you and Mags went to school together." It really was a small world.

"Yes. We're closer than we realized."

I swallowed past the lump in my throat. "You'd be what…seven years older than my mother?"

He nodded. "We might have gone to the same school, but we wouldn't have run into each other."

I locked gazes with him while the others

watched in stunned silence. "Why come forward now?"

"None of the people directly affected are around any longer. I did meet my mother before she took ill. I stopped visiting when you moved in, then she no longer knew who I was."

I was glad he had a relationship with her, if short-lived. "So, it truly is a coincidence that you arrived as trouble started?"

"Yep." He gave a lopsided grin. "Reconnecting with Mags here was frosting on the cake. I intended to rent a house and get to know you a bit before revealing who I was. That didn't work out the way I planned."

I glanced at number ten. Lights burned in all the windows. A large shadow passed behind a pulled-down blind. "That house. Give it time, and it'll be empty. Of course, you don't need it now."

"Nope. I'm content to stay in the house I grew up in."

"Well, this has been a day." Mags scratched her head. "My mind is whirling like a ride at the county fair. I truly hope you aren't using me to get close to CJ."

He put his hand over hers. "Not a chance, my love. Why do you think I've never married?"

I glanced at Eric. He smiled, his eyes warm. We weren't the only romance growing.

"Now what?" Mags asked.

I shrugged. "Keep trying to stay alive and see if we can find out whose foot matches that print. Tell me you took a photo, Ann."

"Of course."

"Mind sharing what you and Davis talked about?" I forked some fried rice into my mouth, hunger returning now that the chat with Larry was over. It would take some time for me to get used to the idea of an uncle. Nice, though, that I wasn't the only one of my bloodline still alive.

"I'm still on probation, but he wants me to keep my eyes open."

"Then why be on probation?"

She shrugged. "I'm getting paid, so it doesn't matter. The only problem is, I don't have access to the information I would have if I were active." She narrowed her eyes at Norma Water's house.

Unless I was mistaken, Ann had the same thing on her mind that I had on mine. She wanted to find a way into that house for some shoes.

I cleared my throat, attracting her attention. When she glanced at me, I nodded.

She gave a knowing smile. We both knew what the next step to tracking down those people would be. I dug into the rest of the food on my plate with gusto. Indecision robbed me of my appetite, while the opposite fueled it.

"I don't like it." Eric shook his head. "You two are going to break and enter. Ann, you won't be on probation anymore; you'll be outright fired."

"I can cause a distraction," Mags said as if he hadn't spoken. "I'm an old lady. No one will think anything devious about me fainting after a jog."

"Nope. You're not doing that," Larry said.

"Oh, hush. You can keep watch from behind a tree or something." She waved him off.

"Has everyone here gone completely crazy?"

Eric glanced from one to the other. “Davis will have a heart attack if he finds out. Besides, if you do find the matching shoe, how are you going to explain to Davis how you got it?” He raised his eyebrows.

“Simple.” I grinned. “We’ll know exactly who to lay the trap for.”

Chapter Eighteen

Ann, Eric, and I sat outside the next morning lost in our thoughts and stared into our coffee mugs. I could guess what was on their minds because it resembled what was on mine. Today's plan to find the shoe that matched the print under my window.

Only Eric would try to talk me out of such an insane plan, while Ann, torn between her job and keeping me safe, would dart from idea to idea until worked into a frazzle.

I glanced at Caper who for once sat still and watched the morning sun flicker on the lake, if dogs did that sort of thing. She would provide the perfect reason to snoop around number ten. I could let her loose and toss something under the house for her to find, and if someone caught me snooping, I'd say I had gone to fetch her. It could work.

Then, there was Mags and her idea of creating a distraction. Plan B. We'd agreed she'd come over when ready.

I glanced at my watch. Seven a.m. I sighed. Waiting was hard.

What did I actually plan to do when I found a matching shoe? Confront a man who outweighed me by a hundred pounds? Not prone to suicidal actions, I'd let Davis know. Yeah, that was the right thing to do.

I glanced up to see Eric staring at me. "What?"

"There's a lot of nodding and pressing of lips going on. What are you thinking?"

"About tossing a dog treat under number ten." I flashed a grin.

He blinked his gorgeous eyes at me for a second, then smiled. "An excuse to be there."

I tapped my temple with my forefinger. "Always thinking."

"Unfortunately." His eyes twinkled. "I've had a report of a disturbance on the river. I won't be around most of the day."

I was starting to hate the river. "Be careful. That disturbance might be the druggies."

"I'm pretty sure it is. I'm taking another ranger with me. No more going anywhere alone until the people are caught."

Relief flooded through me so hard and fast I sagged in my seat. "Good." I raised my face for a kiss.

Eric didn't disappoint. We'd become so used to Ann's presence we forgot she was there. The kiss was tender and full of promises. He kissed me with more urgency, then pulled away. "Please don't do anything foolish."

Ann scoffed. "Remember who you're talking

to."

He frowned. "Be careful." He turned a stern gaze on Ann. "Don't let anything happen to her."

"I'll guard her with my life."

"You do know I'm right here, right?" I glared from one to the other. "I'm capable of watching out for myself."

They both laughed. I rolled my eyes and went into the house to fetch a dog treat. When I returned, Mags and Larry had arrived. My eyes widened at the cotton-candy velour jogging suit Mags wore.

"Aren't you going to be hot in that getup?"

"It'll make my fainting more believable."

I shook my head. "You'll pass out for real, and we'll have to call an ambulance. You're plan B anyway." I explained about throwing the treat under the house. "If things get tense or my story isn't believed, then you can do your act."

"I still don't like it." Another kiss and Eric climbed into his jeep and left us to either succeed or fail horribly.

Okay. Here we go. I took a deep breath, scooped up Caper, and headed for number ten. Making sure no one watched me, I set the dog down and tossed the treat under the house. My pup didn't disappoint. She leaped from my arms and scampered after the treat.

"Ann, you go to the other side, I'll take this one. She won't be easy, the little scamp. Watch for footprints."

"I'm a trained police officer, not an idiot." She disappeared around one corner of the house, leaving me to go around another.

I studied the ground, noting several large footprints, but none with the pattern on the shoe outside my house. Of course, most people owned more than one pair of shoes. "Caper, come on now. Nothing to find here."

"Or here," Ann said, peering at me from the other side. "Get the dog and let's go."

Someone cleared their throat behind me. "Can I help you?"

I glanced into the stern face of Luke—or was it Mark? "I'm trying to get my dog."

He picked up a small rock, tossed it at Caper. She yelped and came running.

I picked her up and sprang to my feet. "You could have hurt her."

"She's out, isn't she? What was your dog doing under there anyway?" He crossed his massive arms.

"Whatever it is dogs do." I hefted my chin, my head barely reaching his chin. "Are you living here? Because if you are, your name needs to be on the lease."

"I don't sleep here if that's what you're asking."

"Isn't it crowded in there with all three of you?"

"Why all the questions?" His brow lowered. "You're a nosy woman. That's dangerous. People who stick their noses where they don't belong tend to find trouble."

Ann stepped up behind me. "Oh, good, you got her. Ready?" She made a move to step around him.

He blocked her path. "It took both of you to get the dog? Or are you snooping?"

From the road, Mags gave a cry and crumbled to the ground. "Help me. I've fallen and I can't get up."

For crying out loud.

The big man in front of me took the bait and rushed to Mags's side. He helped her up and led her to the porch steps. "You sit right here. I'll get you some water." He hurried into the house.

"I'm not drinking anything that man gives me," she whispered. "I've been poisoned before, and I'm a person who learns from their mistakes. I'm leaving before he returns."

"Hm." I watched the house. "Get up, yell out a 'thank you, I feel better,' and let's get out of here."

"I hurt my knee when I fell. It's going to bruise."

"Can you walk?" I asked.

"I can limp, thank you. I'm going home to rest." She hobbled away from the house and down the road. Larry put an arm around her waist.

Ann and I headed to my place. "We didn't learn anything," I said. "Except those men wear the same size shoe. That isn't enough evidence to do anything with."

"He knows we're trying to find out something. We also can't tie him to the druggies. He wasn't one of the men guarding the fields."

"That we saw." I unlocked my front door and led the way inside. "We ran off too fast to be sure of anything. Let's go back."

She put a hand on my shoulder and spun me around. "Eric isn't here."

"I've been there enough times to know where

to go. Larry can go with us. We'll take the road and walk in. We don't need the river." I stepped back, letting her hand fall to her side. "You don't really think they cart the drugs in and out in canoes, do you?"

"No." She plopped onto the sofa. "This is crazy. I'm sure Davis has a team searching the area. Larry typed the coordinates into his phone. We're not equipped to do this."

I sat next to her. "You're right. We're not good for anything other than staying around here and annoying people. But—" I held up a finger in her face. "Norma and her sons are involved somehow. Just a gut feeling. It's not natural how much time they spend in that tiny house. There must be an ulterior motive."

"Then let's stay close to home and focus on them."

Her tone of voice told me she didn't completely share my opinion, but I'd take what I could get. "I need to get into their house."

"Under what pretense? I'm sure the lease agreement says you have to give notice before entering, right?"

"That hasn't stopped me before."

"You've been lucky. If you get too many complaints, you'll get fired and we'll both be out of a job." She rested her head against the back of the sofa.

"True." I groaned and sprawled out, as limp and wrung out as a used-up dishrag. After I finished my pity party, I checked emails. One from Roy about raccoons in the garbage cans and another about someone wanting to be added to the waiting list for a long-term rental. Easy enough, but as for the raccoons, I had no idea other than emptying the trash each evening rather than wait for morning.

I closed my laptop and stood. "We're on garbage patrol."

"Since when?"

"Since Roy is busy and raccoons are making a mess."

"I'll stick to being a cop if the job is still there when this is all over." Ann groaned and pressed to her feet. "This bodyguard stuff can be a real drag sometimes. What do we do with the garbage?"

"Toss it in the back of the cart and take it to the dumpster at the community entrance. Easy enough, and it's better than sitting in the house all day."

"I suppose." She followed me to the cart and off we went.

The trash cans sat strategically around the grounds, partially camouflaged by bushes and flowers. Who wanted to look at places people tossed their garbage? Most of the time. I picked up a fast-food wrapper and tossed it in the bin before removing the lid and hefting out a bag.

Ann took the trash from me and put it in the cart. "Whew. This smells."

"Food that's been sitting out in the summer sun tends to do that."

The third can showed evidence of the four-legged, masked critter's vandalism. Trash lay strewn across the road, under bushes, stuck in branches, and ripped into shreds. The little rascals. I pulled a tool from the cart that helped me pick up litter without having to touch it and went to work.

As they tended to do when I was occupied in a mindless task, my thoughts whirled, settling on Norma Waters and her sons. Big men, big feet, but I'd only seen them wear boots. The footprint near my house clearly showed the imprint of a gym shoe. Her sons could have changed footwear. Gym shoes tended to be quieter than boots, but the soft dirt would have muffled any footsteps.

I didn't have any other suspects. My instinct told me the woman and her sons were involved. The three of them stayed cooped up in that house all day. If they left at all, it had to be after I'd settled in for the night. That seemed strange to me. I glanced at the house in question. The shades were drawn. No yelling, no shadows from lights, nothing.

Wait a minute. *Matt.* I recalled a conversation I'd overheard. Who was Matt and what had happened to him?

"Ann?"

She whipped around from picking up an aluminum can. "Yeah?"

"Did Norma have three sons?"

"Not that I could tell. Why?"

"Matthew, Mark, Luke…what are the odds that she didn't name all her sons after the Gospels. You said her background check was squeaky clean, right? No one is that clean."

"You are." She straightened.

"You did a background check on me?" I quirked an eyebrow.

"Of course. I wanted to know who I was guarding." Her features settled into stone. "You think Waters and her sons aren't what they seem?"

I nodded. "We've had one witness protection, why not more? Or what if they're the ones our victim was running from?"

"Your mind is a scary thing, you know that?"

I grinned. "All we have to do now is prove it." My smile faded when I noticed a grave-faced Davis marching toward us.

Chapter Nineteen

"Where's Eric?" He asked.

"Investigating a disturbance on the river with another ranger." My heart leaped into my throat. "Why? Is something wrong?"

He chewed the inside of his cheek for a moment before answering. "Some canoers said they heard gunfire. Not the kind you'd hear from hunting. Automatic-type gunfire." I could see the effort it took for him to tell me. "I don't want you to worry, CJ. He's probably nowhere near the shooting."

"You know he'd head right for it." I darted for the cart. "I'm going out there."

"Hold on." Davis caught up with me and spun me around to face him. "You can't."

"I know where he might be."

"Where's Larry?"

I shrugged him off. "Off with Mags, no doubt. I'm going with or without you. You'll have to arrest me to stop me."

He sighed. "Since you're my best hope of finding him, I don't have a choice. But, you'll do what I say when I say it. Understood?"

I nodded and climbed into the cart. With Ann beside me and Davis holding onto the back, we sped to my house and his car where he radioed Milton to meet us at the exit point to the river. I could have told Davis the coordinates, but then he wouldn't have let me go. Eric might need me.

After half an hour of driving, I pulled up the coordinates and handed Ann, who sat in the front seat with Davis, my phone. "There is also a tracker that should get us to two hundred yards from Eric if his phone is turned on."

Davis shot me a hard look in the rearview mirror. "You are a devious woman."

I shrugged. "A girl's gotta do what a girl's gotta do." Nothing would stop me from going to Eric. I'd saved him before, I could do it again. Of course, he'd come to my rescue before, too. It's what we did

The parking lot was empty except for Milton's car. He climbed out as we pulled up, frowning when he saw me. Milton opened the trunk of his car and tossed me a vest. "If you're coming, put this on."

"What if they shoot me in the head?" I donned the vest.

"The bullet will ricochet back to them."

"Ha ha." Fear riffled through me despite my flippant attitude. One or more of us could die today. I patted my pockets. Drat. I'd forgotten my Taser and pepper spray in my rush.

"Here." Ann tossed me my purse. "I hope you don't get close enough to use them."

"You grabbed my purse?"

"I figured you'd forget." Her cop face slipped into place. "Stay behind me at all times. If captured, do whatever it takes to stay alive."

I felt as if I were in a badly written action movie. I nodded and stuffed my "weapons" into whatever pocket they'd fit in. I also hoped I wouldn't get close enough to use them.

With Davis in the lead, then Ann, then me, followed by Milton, all wearing Kevlar vests, we hiked toward the coordinates on my phone. An eerie silence surrounded us as if the forest mourned for something terrible. Gunfire meant violence and death. I learned that firsthand with the death of my cousin in a drive-by shooting that happened at the wrong house. I swore I'd never use a gun.

Davis held up his fist in the universal signal to stop. We froze.

I strained my ears to hear, relaxing only when a bird twittered from the tree above us. I glanced up to see a blue jay, his colors striking against the green. Beauty still existed among the evil actions of man.

"Wait." Davis turned toward the water. "This shows Eric is around here somewhere."

Hope replaced fear. I searched the area. Under bushes, around trees. Behind a boulder is where I found a dead man. "Eric," I hissed. "Davis."

Davis hurried toward me. "Ranger, Trailor?." He slowly turned in a circle.

"Here." A hand appeared from a bush, then

Eric sat up, a rag tied around his shoulder.

I dropped to my knees beside him. “Why didn’t you come home?”

“I wanted them to think I was dead, and I couldn’t leave him.” He winced, pointing at Trailor. “I heard them say they’d be back to remove the bodies. When I heard y’all, I thought it was them and crawled in here.”

“Then, let’s get moving.” Milton put his shoulder under Eric’s good arm. “We’ll have to send someone back for Ranger Trailor.”

“I’ll carry him.” Davis slung the other man over his shoulder, grunting under the weight. “Let’s go. I’ll take up the rear this time.”

I stayed close to Eric. He didn’t wear a vest. Hopefully, between Ann, Milton, and me, we could protect him. I wanted to ask questions but held them back until later. Talking would only alert anyone close to our location.

Davis stumbled behind us. “Don’t stop. Keep going.”

“We can’t leave you,” Ann said. “Put him down. We’ll prop him up between us and drag him.”

“His feet will leave a trail.” I swallowed back the mountain in my throat. We were wasting time.

“Doesn’t matter.” She helped Davis lower him. “We’ve got to pick up the pace.”

The roar of four-wheeler engines rose in the distance.

“Oh, no.” I practically dragged Eric and Milton with me. Tears sprang to my eyes when the vehicles came into sight. Eric was placed in the back seat of

Davis's car. Milton took the dead man. Davis spun gravel speeding from the lot, following Milton's car.

I glanced in the rearview mirror to see three men on four-wheelers emerge from the trees. They raised automatic weapons and fired.

I covered Eric with my body.

Ann gasped.

David pressed the accelerator and sent us rocketing away. "Anyone hit?"

"I am." Ann groaned. "That's going to leave a mark."

"Vest?"

"Yeah. They got me in my right shoulder. It's numb, but I'm alive and not bleeding."

I wish I could say the same for Eric. He'd grown paler and lay against me with his eyes closed.

Davis turned on the sirens, clearing drivers from the freeway. "Hold on, Eric. We'll be at the hospital in twenty minutes. Ann, call ahead and tell them what's coming."

Two gurneys, each with two interns, waited at the emergency room entrance. Eric was loaded onto to one, and I ran behind as they wheeled him away.

One of them stopped me in front of two swinging doors. "You'll have to wait in the waiting room, ma'am. The doctor will be out when he has news."

I stood, arms limp at my sides, and watched through the narrow glass panes as they wheeled my man out of sight. I blinked back tears, my legs trembling now that the adrenaline started to wear off. Strange how quickly the rush of relief gave rise to exhaustion.

A nurse led us to the waiting room. "Can I get you officers anything? Coffee?"

I glanced at the vest I wore, noticing for the first time that Police was written across it in big white letters. "Coffee? Cream and sugar."

"Make that four. CJ, help me out of this vest so I can look at my shoulder," Ann asked.

I did, and she rotated her arm. "That hurts, but it'll heal. No need to see a doctor." She glanced up when Milton joined us.

I lowered into a peach-colored vinyl chair and stared idly at a television turned to a news channel with the volume muted. I'd somehow managed to stay out of the news. If I helped bring down someone as big as a drug lord, would that still hold true? Plastering my face across the television would make me a target for every weirdo in the county. Not that I wasn't already surrounded by kooks in the community.

In a vain attempt to keep my mind off Eric, I focused on Norma Waters. I'd bet Caper's collar that wasn't her real name. The problem was finding out who she really was. We'd need DNA or fingerprints. I tapped a finger against my lips, stopping when the nurse handed me a coffee. "Thanks."

When she left, Davis narrowed his eyes at me. "What's going on in that head of yours?"

"I'm trying to think of a way to get Norma Waters' fingerprints." I blew on the hot drink.

"Why?" He drew out the word.

"Because I think she's a fraud."

"CJ thinks because the woman never leaves her house she's not whom she claims to be." Ann rolled her shoulder again. "I checked her out. Norma's clean."

Davis thought for a minute. "People can make up new identities with complete background information. All they need to do is know the right people. How do you plan on doing this?"

"I don't know yet. It isn't as if I can knock on her door and offer her a drink of water."

It seemed an eternity, but in less than two hours, the doctor arrived. "Mr. Drake is out of surgery and doing fine. We've removed the bullet and stitched up the wound. He's awake if you'd like to see him. Since you're all police officers, I'll waive the two-persona-at-a-time rule."

The other three looked at me. I grinned and sailed after the doctor. I didn't mind being mistaken as an officer. Rushing to Eric's side, I placed a gentle kiss on his cheek. "Thank you for not dying."

"My pleasure." His eyes fluttered open.

The other three stood at the foot of the bed. "Feel like talking?" Davis asked.

"Sure. The sooner we catch these guys the better." Eric pushed the button to raise the bed until he was halfway to a sitting position. "I'm on pain meds, so you'll have to make this quick before I drift off."

"Trailor and I went out to investigate the reports of a disturbance. When we arrived, we found a few teenage boys hooting and hollering around a campfire. We assumed they were the disturbance. They weren't. The boys went on to tell us of loud four-wheelers and hunting sounds. Since it isn't hunting season, we told them to head home, and we left to find the source of the shooting. We did." He took a deep breath.

"We reached the fields, which were being plowed over. What could be salvaged was loaded onto trucks. Didn't take a genius to see they were picking up and pulling out. Trailor and I slunk back. We hadn't gone three hundred yards before we heard the four-wheelers after us. Well, you know the rest. They shot at us. Trailor was killed. I hid and prayed CJ would sound an alarm." He smiled at me.

"She didn't," Davis said. "We had more reports of gunfire by canoers."

"I wouldn't have become worried until you didn't show up after dark," I said. "Or if you didn't send me a text."

His brow creased. "How did you find me anyway?"

"I memorized the coordinates when Larry held up his phone the day we found the fields. I put them in my phone. Plus, we had the tracking app. I'm glad you kept your phone on."

"Me too." He closed his eyes. "If those people leave, we'll not find them again."

"I'm requesting a team from Little Rock to go to the area," Davis said. "That's the best I can do at this point. You concentrate on getting well and leave the rest to me."

"Gladly. I'm in no shape to respond to calls anyway."

“You can stay with me.” I caressed his cheek. “I’ll have a bed brought in.”

He laughed, then grimaced. “Your house is way too small.”

“We’ll make it work.” I gave him another kiss and sat in the nearby chair. “Go home, Ann, and feed Caper. No one will harm us here.”

“Not with me outside the door,” Milton said. “You can relieve me in the morning.”

Ann nodded. “Do not leave the hospital under any circumstances without Milton.”

“I won’t.” I didn’t plan on doing anything but find out who Norma really was and to sleep right there until Eric could come home.

Chapter Twenty

I sat upright the next morning and rubbed the sleep from my eyes. I knew what to do next.

"You're awake." Ann stepped into the room and handed me a large frozen, blended coffee.

"Thanks. I figured out how to get Norma's fingerprints."

"How?" She sat in the chair while I perched on the edge of Eric's hospital bed.

"Diet soda cans. Tell me the garbage is still there."

She shook her head. "Roy had Danny clean it up."

Always a wall to bang my head against. "I still need to go through Norma's trash. An aluminum can would have a fingerprint, right?"

"Yes. Do you want me to call Milton to go check?"

"No. I'm going dumpster diving." I gave a sleeping Eric a quick kiss and a promise to return as soon as possible. “She drinks diet soda.”

“She isn’t the only one in the community who does.”

“Then we’ll send every diet soda can to the lab. Come on.” I scowled. “I’ll have to wait until Milton can relieve me. We don’t want to leave Eric unguarded.”

“No, we don’t.” Poor Milton. He’d probably just settled into bed. “Try Davis.”

“Try me for what?” Davis strolled into the room. “I’d hoped Eric was awake so he could tell me more about the men who shot him.”

“Great.” I flashed a grin. “Ann and I have some garbage to tend to.” I waved and hurried out of the room before he could stop me. He’d watch over Eric until Ann and I returned.

Ann hurried to the dumpsters in front of the community, then handed me a pair of latex gloves from the glove compartment. “This is a disgusting idea.”

“You’ve never had to go inside a dumpster as a cop? They do all the time on TV.”

“This isn’t a television crime show.” She rolled her eyes and snapped her gloves into place.

“Why don’t you stand guard and I’ll do the dirty work.” I shoved my door open.

“That’s the best idea you’ve had in a long time. Make it quick, okay? People are going to start leaving for work.”

“Got it covered. Give me a boost.” I stepped into her cupped hands. “I lost a ring.”

“You don’t wear jewelry.” She hefted me up and over. “I’ll knock if someone’s coming.”

"Whoa." I flew over the top and landed in something squishy. Gross. "Not so hard next time, and no one will notice whether I wear jewelry or not."

"I really hope there isn't a next time, CJ."

To be honest, I shared her hope. Getting involved in dangerous situations got old fast. I glanced down to see what I'd landed in and promptly threw up.

"What is it?"

"A dead raccoon, bloated and disgusting." My stomach heaved again. I was going to kill Roy if he had anything to do with the animal's death. Digging in trash was not a criminal offense or I'd be in jail soon.

"Move it aside and start digging. We don't have all day, and you're going to need a shower before we return to the hospital."

No truer words ever spoken. I picked up the poor animal by the tail and placed it in the furthest corner of the dumpster. Two feet away didn't remove the smell far enough from my nose.

Mentally apologizing to the waste management crew, I ripped open garbage bags and stacked diet soda cans. Ann pounded on the dumpster. I ducked and froze.

Seconds later, a bag landed on my head and burst open, covering me with leftover spaghetti and meatballs. Could the day get any worse? Yep. A bag of dog pooh came next. This was a bad idea.

Another knock from Ann signaled the coast was clear. I started tossing out cans. Hopefully, one of them had been handled by Norma. I couldn't stay in the dumpster any longer.

Ann knocked.

I ducked.

Roy cursed and tossed the cans back into the dumpster.

I stood and poked my head over the top. "I need those."

He yelped and jumped back, his hand over his heart. "What in tarnation are you doing in there?"

"Collecting cans."

A serious look came over his face. "Do you need a loan? You won't earn much from recycling these."

"Police business." Ann stepped from around the dumpster. "Help her out of there, please."

I tossed the cans back out and reached up my hands. "Gently."

Roy grabbed my hands and dragged me out. I landed not so softly onto the pavement. "Lord, girl, you reek." He stumbled back.

"You aren't riding in my car until you've cleaned up," Ann said, holding her nose.

"Fine. But first, I want to know why there's a dead animal in the dumpster." I planted hands on my hips and gave Roy my sternest look.

"I found it dead on the side of the road. It's been there a few days. I didn't think you'd want it to gross out your tenants, so I scooped it up and threw it away.

I stomped my way home, despite Ann's protests about going without her and left it up to her to load the cans into her car.

After glancing around to make sure no one

could see me, I stripped off my foul-smelling clothes on the front porch and entered the house in my underwear. Caper gave a welcoming whine, sniffed, and darted under the sofa with her tail between her legs. I guess my pup didn't like the scent of death.

"Sorry girl. You aren't allowed in the hospital. I promise to make it up to you." I stepped into the shower, finished undressing, and stood under the hot spray until the water turned cold.

"Hurry up, CJ." Ann pounded on the door. "We need to drop these cans off with Milton. Davis is having a fit because we aren't back yet."

I stepped out, wrapped in a towel, and climbed the stairs. "Ten minutes. Would you mind taking Caper out?"

"Why don't you ask Mags to watch her until you come back?"

"The cat hates her." I pulled out a pair of skinny jeans and a tank top from my closet and got dressed. Sweeping my hair into a ponytail, I doused myself with a floral cologne and rejoined Ann outside.

"That's better." She handed me Caper.

"I feel better." I put the dog back in the house, apologized for leaving again, and followed Ann to the car. As usual, I couldn't help but glance at number ten.

Mark and Luke stood on the postage-stamp lawn, arms folded, and watched.

I waved and climbed into Ann's car. "They suspect us as much as we suspect them."

"Yep. Not good." She turned the car around

and drove to Milton's.

When he didn't answer the doorbell, she set the bag of cans on his porch, left a note, and returned to the hospital after stopping for a dozen doughnuts. Cliché, but my stomach protested missing breakfast.

Davis sprang to his feet, relief on his face when we returned. "Thank goodness. Eric keeps drifting in and out of sleep, I'm hungry, have work to do, and hate hospitals." He snatched a chocolate-glazed doughnut.

"Did he tell you anything more?" Ann set the box on the bedside table.

"Big, Caucasian, dark hair—the description fits a lot of people." He frowned in my direction. "Fragrance works best when applied with a soft touch."

"Don't ask." I took a glazed twist and sat in the chair.

"She needed it, believe me," Ann added. "I left a bag of cans on Milton's doorstep to be taken to the lab. We're hoping to get a print off one of them for Norma Waters and her goons."

His eyes widened. "Good thinking. I'll pick them up on my way to the station. I already regret saying this, but you'd make a good detective, CJ." He left me with my mouth hanging open, stopped at the door and glanced back. "Except for your recklessness." He stepped into the hall, his footsteps echoing on the marble floors.

"High praise, indeed." Ann gave a sardonic smile.

"He is incapable of complimenting me without also insulting me." I took Eric's hand in mine, stroking the back of it with my thumb.

Eric's eyes flickered open. "Water, please." He pressed the button to raise the bed.

I held the cup with a bendable straw to his mouth. "How are you feeling?"

"Like I've been shot." The corner of his mouth twitched. His nose wrinkled. "A little heavy with the cologne, sweetheart."

His eyes grew larger and larger as I told him of our morning adventure. "Wow. Glad I missed it."

"I'm not." Mags stood in the doorway, arms crossed, tears in her eyes. "Why do you insist on investigating without me? Why did I have to hear about Eric from Davis when I called to see where you were last night? Why did I hear about you dumpster diving from Roy? I thought we were partners."

"I'm sorry." I rushed to hug her. "It was a split-minute decision to go find Eric. I spent the night here and got the idea of looking for fingerprints on soda cans this morning."

She sniffed. "Larry and I are capable of helping, you know."

"I know, but time was of the essence. Have a doughnut." I handed her the box.

"Sugar doesn't help." She chose a cream-filled. "Larry is buying sodas from the cafeteria. Anyone want anything?" When we shook our heads, she took the chair I'd vacated. "What's next?"

"We wait for fingerprint results," Ann said. "Davis will put a rush on it."

"Since you suspect Norma Waters, have your tried facial recognition? It's the new thing."

"I doubt it." Ann typed into her phone. "We've only now suspected her of anything."

"Good idea, Mags." I smiled.

"See? I've a good head on my shoulders. In fact, Luke—or was it Mark—anyway, he came by to check on me after my fainting spell. If his mother is a crook, she raised a good son."

"A cover-up." I sat on the foot of Eric's bed. "They're all guilty."

"Harsh considering you have no solid evidence." Mags frowned.

"Just because the man helped an old lady doesn't make him a saint."

"Watch who you call old, young lady. You're already treading on eggshells with me." She hefted her chin.

Eric chuckled, obviously amused by our argument. "You two are something else. Are you sure you aren't mother and daughter?"

"I hope not," Larry said, carrying in two large Styrofoam cups. "Mags would be my sister." He shuddered. "That would be a whole new crime." He gave her a kiss.

The nurse came in and ran us out for a few minutes. We congregated outside Eric's room while she checked his bandage and vitals.

"Our police force needs more people." I leaned against the wall.

"Thinking of joining?" Ann crooked a brow.

"Heavens no. But if we had more, someone else could guard Eric's room and we could find out who's behind whoever shot him. Staying here is wasting time." I wanted the person who tried to kill my man to pay.

The elevators at the end of the hall opened. Luke stared out at us, then pressed the button to close the door.

"Hey." I dashed for the elevator, reaching it just as the doors closed too much to squeeze through. All I could see was the hard glint in the man's eyes.

Chapter Twenty-One

It took two days for the fingerprints and facial recognition to come back. Davis sat across from me at the picnic table and slid a folder across the wood top.

My fingers trembled as I opened the folder and stared at the face of Norma Lake. "She didn't venture far from her name, did she?" I glanced at number ten. I'd woken that morning to find it empty. Video cameras recorded a van, and the Waters family filling it with their possessions.

"Her husband was the man Robert Evans put behind bars. It appears she's taken over his operation."

"Her sons?"

"Three. The oldest, Matthew, was found dead six months ago in an alley. We chalked it up to a mugging, but considering what you heard, I'm thinking his family killed him."

"Now what?"

"We keep searching."

I slid the folder back. "They'll come after me or Eric."

He nodded. "Most likely. You do attract violent people."

"Any idea where they'll be hiding?"

"No. I'm sorry. The danger isn't over yet."

I should have stayed out of this one. Too late now. I'd step out as bait and end this.

"I know what you're thinking and don't do it. They may stay away."

I narrowed my eyes. "That is a slim possibility, and you know it. They're hiding in the mountains waiting to strike."

"What purpose would they have in killing you?"

"Pay back for digging into their past." I watched crime shows when I could. I knew criminals had no code of justice and didn't value life. Mine would be just another notch on their belt. Nothing more.

"I'm putting you under house arrest. If you leave this community for any reason, I'll lock you up." He pushed to his feet and tucked the folder under his arm. "Lowery, I mean it. If you have any chance of getting your job back, you will make sure she stays put."

I leaped to my feet. "What about Eric?"

"He's being released in the morning. You can do without him for one day. Why don't you concentrate on getting a bed ready for him?" Back stiff, he strode to his car.

"That's police brutality. You can't lock me up.

I've done nothing wrong." I stomped my foot.

He climbed in the car and rolled down the window. "Interfering in a police investigation is what I'll say to keep you safe." He rolled the window up and sped off.

Hands on my hips, I spun to face Ann. "You won't keep me here, will you?"

"Sorry, but yes. You heard him. I have to if I want my job back."

"You seesaw about things more than I do. Make up your mind about whether you want to be a cop or not." I stormed into the house and slammed the door.What was I supposed to do with myself? I couldn't go see Eric, I couldn't try to find the Lake family…nothing!

"You're acting like a spoiled child." Ann came in the house and did her own door slamming.

My tiny house shook as if a strong wind blew outside. "So what?" I plopped onto the sofa.

"You like it here. Unless you're involved in something you shouldn't be, you're perfectly content to stay on these grounds."

True, but I wasn't ready to give in yet. "I guess I should go clean out number ten again." I should leave the darn house empty and never rent it again.

"That's the spirit." She reopened the front door.

Caper ran out as if she were the one on house arrest. I followed at a more sedate pace, trying to concoct a plan to thwart Ann and Davis that wouldn't get me killed. Not wanting Mags to feel left out this time, I stopped at her house first.

"Want to go with me to check out number

ten?"

She straightened from her flower bed and pushed back her straw hat. "Empty again?"

"Yep. They skipped out sometime during the night."

"Why aren't you at the hospital?"

I scowled. "House arrest."

"Oh." Her brows rose. "This is something I want to hear. Yes, I'll go with you." She hopped on the back and held on.

A few minutes later, I stood looking at a house that was as clean as the day Norma and her sons had moved in. Not a speck of paper, aluminum can—nothing that could be linked to them. We were not dealing with dummies. I still searched every corner for evidence and wasn't surprised when I didn't find any. I'd managed to use up an hour of my prison time.

"You poor thing." Mags patted me on the shoulder and gave Ann what my grandfather would have called a roadkill look. "That woman told me all about what Davis said. Don't you worry. I intend to speak to Amber right away about her boyfriend."

"What is wrong with you two?" Ann shook her head. "It's as if you both have a death wish."

"No, just a desire to help the local authorities and see justice done. Right?"

I nodded. "That sums it up."

"God help me, I'm surrounded by wannabe vigilantes." Ann marched to the cart and climbed on the back. "Any other work to pass the time?"

I wished. "Let's go check the chapel. It's been a while." Maybe we'd see signs of the Lakes having been there, although the idea of them stepping foot in a church was ludicrous. “It needs a weekly dusting and sweeping. We can do that.”

“Great. Now I’m a maid,” Ann yelped when I pressed the gas a little too hard. “Not funny.”

I smiled, thinking it funny indeed. I parked at the top of the trail and collected the cleaning supplies from behind the seat. “This will take at least another hour.” Tomorrow, I’d have Eric to take care of.

While the other two dusted, I swept, occasionally glancing out the glass walls to see whether anyone watched us. The hair on my arms stayed in place. The day promised to drag. I had no more ideas on how to pass the time or how to ditch Ann. Not that I knew where to go, at least not yet. Maybe some time on my laptop would make something pop.

When we’d finished at the chapel, Mags ordered me to stop at Amber’s. “Her car is here, which means she’s home.” She hopped out and knocked on the front door.

“Why are you knocking?” Amber asked, opening the door. “I’ve told you before to walk in.”

“I don’t want to enter into an embarrassing situation.” Mags stepped inside and waved for Ann and me to join her. We filled the tiny-house living room despite Amber’s minimal decorating style.

“I want you to tell Davis to leave CJ alone.” Mags wasn’t one to hold back.

“I don’t get involved in his job, Grandma.” Amber crossed her legs. “We’ve gone over this before. “Bill has CJ’s best interest at heart. We all know her propensity to walk face first into danger."

"How's Eric?" I was tired of people saying how much I attracted trouble.

"He's good. Ready to get out of the hospital. Milton is tired of playing guard and not happy that Ann can't relieve him anymore."

Another reason to get this over with, but what did I know? "Does he need a ride home tomorrow?"

She shook her head. "I'll bring him."

Drat. Foiled again. "All right. I've work to do. Ann?" I rose to my feet.

"I'm coming." She followed me out. Mags had decided to visit awhile. Nag was probably more like it. She'd be like a gnat trying to persuade Amber to tell her something vital or to convince Davis to change his mind. I wished her luck.

At home, I pulled down the fold-up table on the wall, opened my laptop, and set a pad of paper and a pen next to it. Time to do some serious research.

Ann sat across from me to do the same thing. "This is the safe way to find a killer."

"Hush." I typed in Norma Lake and got to work.

By suppertime, my head ached and my eyes crossed. I managed to find some news articles, but I bet the library would've had more information. The most important discovery was where they lived when Robert Evans had turned on them. Twenty miles up Highway 105 at the base of the mountain. I'd bet the wheels off my house they'd returned to the land where they'd once grown marijuana. They wouldn't be dumb enough to move back in the house, but the mountain offered plenty of places to hide.

I needed a way out of here without leaving Eric in danger. If I snuck out, which wasn't going to be easy, Ann would stay with Eric. She'd protect whoever was closest. Then again, I didn't want to face down a gun-wielding drug lord without armed protection. Quite the dilemma.

"Stop shooting daggers at me and write down what you find so we can pass it on to Davis." Ann returned my glare. "I'm doing my job."

I curled my lip. Eric would know more about where three people could live in the forest. The trick would be persuading him to tell me.

"Stop trying to formulate a way of escaping. I'm going to be watching you like a junkyard guard dog. One little trick and I'm going to have you arrested."

"Whatever do you mean? I've been well-behaved all day."

"That's what worries me."

Mags yanked open the front door and burst inside. "Guess what Amber let slip?" She shot a steely look at Ann. "Go outside. You'll tell Davis."

"I will not." Ann crossed her arms and leaned back in her chair.

"Will not what? Leave or tell Davis?"

Ann's answer was a sly smile.

"Oh, forget it." Mags left, but not before putting her hand to her ear in the universal way of saying "call me."

I texted her instead. *Tell me.*

Amber said Davis talks in his sleep. She said that he believes the Lakes are on the mountain. He's been talking to Eric about where.

Well, pooh. I'd figured that out for myself. *Tell me something I don't know.*

Mags wrote more. *Amber didn't tell me this, but I know where an abandoned hunter's cabin is.* □

Talk to you later. Am erasing this conversation. I ended the text and erased the texts in my phone's trashcan. I grinned at Ann. "She doesn't know anything. Mags was just trying to get you riled."

"Uh huh. That's why you went back and forth a few times. Do I need to put a leash on you?"

Which reminded me, Caper hadn't been out in a while. I stood and opened the front door. "Come on, girl."

"Me first." Ann jumped up and stood between me and the outside. "I'm wearing my vest."

"Good for you. Always prepared." I needed to chill or she'd grow more suspicious. One way or the other, I was going up the mountain without her. Better yet, I'd leave a trail so she could follow me with her gun, bringing Milton and Davis with her. I had a plan. A stupid plan, but a plan nonetheless.

I wanted my life back. I sat in the chair on the porch, while Ann stood between me and the railing. "I'm not too excited about having your rear two inches from my face."

"Too bad."

I leaned as far over as I could without falling to see my dog staring across the lake. "What's up with Caper?"

Ann shrugged. "No idea. She's doing what she does best, nothing."

"No, that isn't her normal posture. Look. Her hackles are up." I glanced across the lake.

The sun glinted off something.

I tackled Ann to the ground as a shot was fired.

Caper went into a frenzy of barking.

"Get inside." Ann shoved me off her. "Crawl."

"Come, Caper." I scurried inside like a crawdad, slamming and locking the door as soon as Ann's feet cleared the doorframe.

"Thanks, CJ. How did you know?" Ann scooted her back against the wall.

"Remember those annoying sunglasses Luke and Mark wore?"

She nodded.

"I'm pretty sure it was one of them taking a sniper shot at us." They weren't far away at all. I ducked my head to hide my smile. *I'm coming for you.*

Chapter Twenty-Two

I waited anxiously for Eric's arrival, covering the four steps from one end of my porch to the other. Roy had brought in a rather comfortable cot and placed it under the front window. The house was snug, but my man was worth the inconvenience.

"I wish you'd wait inside. The shooter might not miss next time." Ann glared with crossed arms, her cop face in place.

"I'm too excited." I jumped off the porch and rushed to Amber's car as it stopped next to my house. "You're here." I yanked open the door.

"I am." Eric, looking tired and a little pale, smiled up at me. With a groan, he got out of the car, refusing my help. "I won't get stronger unless I do things for myself."

"You're here so I can help you."

"I'll let you know when I need help." He gave me a quick kiss. "No offense, sweetheart."

"All right. You're a big tough man." I relented, staying behind him as he climbed the porch steps. I wanted to carry him and wait on him hand and foot. That bullet could have stolen him from me.

Eric lowered himself to the cot. "Are you blaming yourself?"

I shook my head.

"Liar. Come here." He patted the mattress next to him. "I got shot doing my job."

"You're a forest ranger. You shouldn't be shot at." I sat and leaned my head on his good shoulder.

"You're right. My job is supposed to be easy and threat-free, but I still deal with people. They can be anything but." He kissed the top of my head.

"You could've been killed."

"Yes, and my friend was."

"Did CJ tell you someone took a shot at her from across the lake yesterday?" Ann pretended to study her nails.

"Traitor." I gave her a look that should've shut her up.

"She saw the glint from something and tackled me to the porch. Saved my life, I suppose, but she refuses to listen to reason and stay in the house."

I pushed to my feet. "That isn't much safer. If you'll recall, someone barricaded the door and set fire to my porch." I still needed Roy to replace the scorched boards so I wouldn't have the daily reminder. "If they wanted me dead, I'd be dead already."

"Hold on." Eric put a hand on my arm. "Sit back down, sweetheart. Let me think." He rubbed a hand down his face. "You're right. You should be dead by now. What changed? What made someone shoot at you? Did the bullet come close enough or was it a warning?"

"It would have taken one of us down if CJ hadn't noticed." Ann leaned her elbows on her knees. "They aren't giving warnings anymore."

"Again, what changed? CJ isn't a threat to them."

"I'm not?" I frowned. "I'm the one who revealed their true identity."

"Yes, but the circle's widening. They'd have to get rid of all of us, including the local police force. Davis has probably spread the word to Little Rock and the FBI."

"So, it's just plain ole revenge for me sticking my nose into their business."

He nodded. "Wouldn't be the first time a drug lord offed someone as an example. We live in a small town. Killing you tells everyone else to not meddle. Drugs have been a problem for as long as you've been alive. Moonshine, pot—there will always be someone breaking the law."

I sighed. "Davis needs to hurry up and catch the guys. I have a job to do. It's time to drive around the community and see if anything needs attention."

"You'll be a duck in a shooting gallery," Ann said. She got up and closed the curtains, making me feel more like a prisoner. "Roy can handle things for a few days."

"It's been weeks." I flounced back, hitting my head on the wall. "Ow." I rubbed the sore spot.

"That's what throwing a fit will get you." Ann

smiled and turned her attention to her phone. "Why don't you watch TV or something and let Eric rest?"

He did look tired. I stood so he could stretch out. "Do you need anything?"

"Water would be fine." He closed his eyes. "I'll think of something, sweetheart. Give me time."

I nodded, filled a glass with water, and set it within his reach before taking a seat next to Ann. My phone showed no messages as usual, so I slipped my cell into my pocket, then picked up the remote to change the channel to a true-crime cable show. I propped my feet on the chest in front of me.

The narrative explained the background to the story, about how a suspect on house arrest escaped through a hole in the floor. The man went on to commit several more crimes. I eyed the hidden storage door. It wouldn't work. I'd make too much noise pulling out everything I'd stored there.

If I did find a way out, what would I do then? I wasn't a tracker so couldn't find signs of whoever shot at me, then follow them to their hideout. The only idea I had, and it was a stupidly dangerous one, was to make myself a target and hope they took me captive rather than kill me. Only thing—they had no reason to take me captive.

I wouldn't be good as a bargaining chip. No money, no property other than Grams's house. No way of convincing the authorities to let the Lakes go. I'd be collateral damage at best.

"The TV isn't going to give you any good ideas," Ann said.

"Why not? They're true stories."

"Just sit tight. Davis has a search party heading up the mountain. They'll find the Lakes, and this will be over. Life can then resume to normal."

"They're out searching?" Good news. Maybe it would be over soon. "I guess you're ready to move into the house."

"More than ready. I'm starting to feel like a lab rat here. No offense."

"None taken." I was ready for my house back.

Leaving the television on, I pulled up last night's video recordings and idly flipped through the frames. Every time the motion sensor was triggered, the device recorded the movement.

Mark Lake appeared, strolling down the road of Heavenly Acres, rifle in hand, as if he didn't have a care in the world. I glanced at the time stamp. Just past one a.m. What in the world was he doing there? I switched screens to see him slide under my car.

"Ann." I pointed.

"What's he doing?"

I shrugged. "It can't be good."

"Stay here." She donned her Kevlar vest, grabbed her gun, and raced out the door.

I parted the curtains enough to peer out.

Ann pulled a flashlight from her pocket and shined it on the undercarriage of the car. When she straightened, the look on her face sent chills to my core. She hurried back into the house.

"What is it?" I let the curtain fall into place.

"Mark Lake put a bomb on your car. My guess is that it's triggered to go off when you start the ignition. I'm calling for a bomb squad."

My knees gave out. I grabbed the edge of the window ledge to keep from falling. If I'd taken the car, I'd be dead. Lesson learned. Sit back and let those who know what they're doing do their job. It wouldn't be easy for a Nosy Nellie like me to rely on others like a fainting violet.

"Those security cameras were well worth the expense," Ann said. "I don't want to think what would've happened if we hadn't found the bomb. The squad is coming from Little Rock. It will take a while. I also texted Davis, but he must have his phone on silence. No response."

I made my way on trembling legs to the sofa. "He wouldn't want a call to alert anyone to his presence." I took a deep breath and exhaled slowly.

"You aren't going to faint, are you?" Worry creased Ann's face.

"No. I don't faint. Just gathering myself."

Mark walked with confidence in last night's video. Yes, most people slept at that time, but someone could've seen and called the authorities. I wasn't quite sure how to handle a killer so confident they didn't care if they were seen. So I decided to take the advice given me over and over and stay in my house.

Eric groaned and sat up, took one glimpse of my face, and asked, "What happened?"

"Someone put a bomb on CJ's car." Ann fetched me a cold soda from the refrigerator. "Bomb squad is on the way."

I told him about the video footage. "I've decided to stay in the house from now on and delegate all responsibilities to Roy."

"Finally, she gets a brain." Ann sat next to me.

We were in this predicament because Caper found a severed finger. I glanced at my dog sleeping peacefully under Eric's cot. Why couldn't I have inherited a lazy dog that didn't care what went on around her?

"Hello?" Mags called, then knocked. "Can I come in?"

Ann opened the door, pulled Mags inside, and locked the door behind her. "Did you see anyone?"

"No, should I have?" She handed me a cake. "I thought Eric might be tired of hospital food so I baked a chocolate cake. What did I miss?"

"My car is bombed. Yum." I set the cake on the counter and searched for a knife. I cut four good-sized pieces and handed a plate to everyone. "This ought to make us feel better."

For a while at least. I sat next to Eric and dug in. An engine rumbled outside, then went quiet. Caper came out from under the bed and moved to the door.

"Wait a bit, girl. I'll take you out after I finish this cake."

"No, you won't," Ann said. "I will."

"If something happens to you, then who will guard CJ?" Mags shook her head. "I'll take the dog out. No one wants to kill me. This is why cats are easier. They don't have to go outside where someone might shoot you."

"Regardless, it's cruel to keep her cooped up inside."

Caper yipped.

"See? She agrees with me."

Caper's yip turned to a full-out bark fest.

"Fine." Mags set down her cake.

"Don't open that door," I said. I recognized my dog's guarding behavior.

Too late. Mags gasped and stumbled back.

Caper sank her teeth into Luke Waters' leg.

I slipped my Taser and pepper spray into a pocket, grateful I'd chosen comfort that day instead of fashion. The baggy gym shorts would hide my protection.

He raised his gun at Ann. "Pull your weapon and I'll shoot one of the others."

She took her hand away from her gun.

One hard shake of his leg sent Caper sliding across the floor.

Luke aimed his weapon at me. "Why couldn't you take a hint and leave things alone?"

Chapter Twenty-Three

"Let's go." He said, motioning his head toward the door. "Make it snappy before someone sees us, or I'll shoot the ranger."

I glanced at Eric, then at the others. I couldn't risk their lives by refusing. "I'm coming, but we can't take my car. Your brother put a bomb on it."

Luke cursed. "He's always been a hothead."

Ann stepped out on the porch as Luke ushered me to a beat-up truck, holding me in front of him like a shield.

"Back off, cop. I've been pushed to my limit. Step back in the house and close the door. Do not attempt to follow." He climbed in the passenger side door, dragging me after him.

From the corner of my eye, I caught a glimpse of Larry pulling into the community. His eyes widened, but he wisely drove past as if he hadn't seen us. Good. He'd follow.

Luke squealed tires as he raced from the

community. “I don’t like to hurt girls, but my brother doesn’t have the same restrictions.”

“Then let me go.” I reached for the door handle.

“If you jump out, I’ll run over you, then go back and kill your boyfriend. I don’t have a problem shooting men.”

“If you hurt my dog, you’ll be sorry.”

“I like dogs, but I’m pretty sure my leg is bleeding.” He increased speed as we hit the interstate. “There’s no way your friends can follow, not even the military man. I’m too fast.” He zipped past a slower moving vehicle.

“Why did you take me?” I turned and faced him. “I’m no good to you.”

“Because Mother insisted.”

My heart dropped to my knees. “Why?”

“It won’t be pleasant.”

I gripped the door handle. I needed to find a way to escape before we reached the rest of his family. My chances would be next to nil with three-against-one odds. “If your mother wants me, then why did Mark put a bomb on my car?”

“He didn’t know. I don’t like talking.”

“Mags seems to think you’re a good guy. Don’t ruin her opinion of you by murdering me.”

A muscle ticked in his jaw. His hands tightened on the wheel.

I needed to keep him talking. All the crime shows said to make your abductor think of you as human, someone important. The only way I could think of was to let him know me better.

So, I held onto the idea of him not liking to

hurt girls and took a chance. "I spent most of my adult life taking care of my grandmother. She died last year. That's when I took over as overseer at Heavenly Acres. I don't mind living in a tiny house. Did you like it?" When he didn't answer, I continued.

"I felt as if taking care of Grams would help me take care of others, know what I mean?" I folded my trembling hands in my lap. "I think I'm good at my job. Caper—that's my dog—I inherited her along with a house. My friend Ann is going to rent it from me. I have to admit the extra income will be nice." *If I'm alive long enough to enjoy the extra money.*

"Mags, the lady you helped up, she's the first friend I met here. She can be a bit abrasive, but I love her. Eric is a dream man. Kind, gentle…well, nothing like you and your brother." *Uh-oh.*

He cut me a glance. "I can be kind."

"If you were, you'd let me go. Is your mother going to torture me? I don't know anything. My dog found a finger. Y'all rented a house from me, that's it."

He focused again on the road.

I sighed. "Mags prefers cats over dogs. I might have to reconsider my first opinion since Caper needing to go out is why I'm in your truck. Of course, you would have found another way. Was it you who tried to shoot me last night? Those stupid sunglasses of yours gave you away."

"The shot was your last warning. Mark wouldn't have missed."

"Well, you did. I tackled my friend to the

ground, thus preventing you from hitting one of us. It came too close, Luke." I shot him a glare. "How much further?"

"Too long if you're going to keep blabbing."

Count on it, buddy. "My parents died when I was a teenager. Grams took over after that, so of course, I took care of her until she died. It's not easy losing loved ones or being an orphan. At least you have your mother." Until the three of them were behind bars. Then, he'd never see her again.

I peered out the window as he veered onto an access road. "I know where we're going." I stared at him. "You three actually went back to the river? Where the fields are? Oh, I get it. Hide in plain sight. I'll have to remember that. If I'm not dead soon. I hope I'll be alive. I'm only twenty-five. Do you know I've never had a real boyfriend before Eric? I've missed out on a lot. I'd really like time to experience what I haven't." A sideways glance showed his jaw tick working overtime.

My idea of babbling on would either work or escalate the danger. I chose to keep talking. If nothing else, it kept me from dwelling on the fear growing inside me. I sighed and tapped my fingers on my leg. *My phone.* Some of the tension left my shoulders. I could be tracked the same way I'd located Eric.

"Do you like living on the mountain or in town? I prefer being outside of town. It's quieter and more peaceful. Was your brother too dumb to know we had security cameras, or didn't he care? Are y'all twins? You could be. Why did Matt die?"

His gaze flickered to me, then back to the road.

"Painful subject? Okay. I won't ask you again, although I did overhear your mother threaten you and Mark with the same thing." I opened the glove compartment. A wicked-looking knife, some wadded-up napkins, nothing else much of interest. "You travel light."

"Do not take the knife. I'm watching you."

If we weren't going so fast down the road, I'd fill his eyes with pepper spray, then tase him for good measure. But, that would result in an accident I might not walk away from. I'd have to bide my time. "I'm thinking of getting me a pink knife. I like pink. What's your favorite color? Do you have any water in the truck? I'm getting thirsty."

"Behind the seat. If you didn't talk so much, your mouth wouldn't be as dry."

True. I got to my knees and grabbed a water bottle from the case. "Want one?"

He shook his head.

"Suit yourself." I settled back in my seat, unscrewed the cap, and took a long swallow. "I'm going to need to use the restroom soon."

"Then I suggest you not drink all that water."

I replaced the cap. "Why don't you feel bad about shooting guys, but you don't like hurting girls? We're all people. We all bleed red. A life is a life. If you feel that strongly about the issue, you really should pull over and let me out."

No answer. I sighed and racked my brain for something else to say. If I was right about our location, our destination wasn't far away. When we passed the parking lot at the exit point, my heart went into overdrive.

"It's pretty out here. Do you like to kayak? It's fun and quite relaxing. A canoe is a little harder but still fun." My throat grew hoarse from the one-sided conversation. "When I was little, I wanted to be a wife and a mother. That's all. Now, I guess I won't get that chance. How is your mother going to torture me? Will she wait until I'm dead before she starts cutting off my fingers and toes? Pulling out my teeth? Hope so because I don't like pain. I'll probably cry, then scream. It'll be horrible." I shuddered. "But I'll try to be brave. I'm not afraid of dying…I've seen enough of it, I just don't want it to hurt. Maybe your brother could just shoot me in the head?"

I envisioned myself fighting back, disabling one or two of them, then glanced at Luke's muscled arms. I'd be no match for one, much less, two of the men. Maybe I could take the mother and threaten her safety in order to escape.

The truck stopped. "We walk the rest of the way."

I jumped out of the truck and took off running. Before I'd gone ten feet, Luke's massive arms swept me off my feet and over his shoulder.

"I had to try. This is an uncomfortable mode of transportation. Put me down or I'll vomit down your back. I promise not to run."

He set me on my feet. "I'm about at my wit's end with you. Run and I'll reconsider not liking to shoot girls."

"Okay." I grinned. "Are you married? I bet you wouldn't look so grim if you smiled."

He spun me around and shoved me forward.

"I should probably follow you since I don't know where I'm going."

"Nope."

Every step we took brought me closer to the end. I crumbled to the ground. "My ankle." When he made a move to pick me up again, I held up my hand. "No, no, just let me rest a minute. I'll limp in on my own two feet." Tears sprang to my eyes as I remembered Eric saying almost those same words when Amber dropped him off.

Be tough, CJ. I pushed to my feet and started walking.

"I thought you hurt yourself," Luke said.

"I lied."

He chuckled.

I whirled. "Did you just laugh? You are human after all." I two-hand shoved him. He didn't move. It was like pushing against a wall and only made him laugh harder.

"I wish we didn't have to kill you."

"That makes two of us." I resumed my march forward, resigned to arriving as quickly as possible and creating a new plan of escape. One that involved hurting one or more people. I'd sneak away, dash through the woods, and hide until rescued. It was a solid plan once I got away.

I froze at the edge of the cleared fields. Now that the plants were gone, I could see the cabin at the other end. Mark stood, rifle in hand, on a ramshackle porch. I stepped closer to Luke in hopes of preventing the other man from shooting me where I stood.

"Come on. There's no sense in delaying the

inevitable." He took my arm and dragged me forward.

I dragged my feet, having changed my mind about getting there quickly. No more words spilled forth. Instead, cotton filled my mouth. I tried swallowing against a dry throat and wished I'd brought along the water bottle. "Can I ask you a favor?" I glanced up at the man who towered over me by a foot.

"What?"

"Have them kill me fast."

He gave a grim nod.

Well, that was something at least. What did his mother hold over him to make him do what he was reluctant to do? No son was that obedient, were they? I'd been a good kid, but even I rebelled when I didn't want to do something.

I planted my feet and faced him. "What's she got against you? I mean, you're a big tough guy. If you don't want to do something, why do it? Don't tell me you're a sissy momma's boy. Oh, I get it. It's okay to kill others, but you don't want to be murdered like your brother. You're a coward." I doubled up my fist and punched him in the jaw, effectively breaking my thumb. I really should have taken those self-defense classes Ann suggested.

Chapter Twenty-Four

I cradled my right hand, nausea roiling in my stomach, then glared up at an amused Luke. "I hate you." I might've liked him under different circumstances, like if he weren't part of a drug manufacturing, killing family.

"You wouldn't be the first." He grabbed my arm again and dragged me across the field. When we reached his mother, he gave me a shove, sending me to my knees.

I stifled back a cry and glared at the woman. "What now?"

"You're a feisty one." Norma smiled without humor. "Bring her into the cabin."

Luke ushered me inside and pointed to a chair in the center of the room. The plastic under my seat didn't fill me with warm fuzzy feelings.

"Why me?" I blinked back tears. My hand throbbed.

"Because you're the one who started all this."

Norma cocked her head. “I thought it might be you. That’s why I rented that stupid box of a house. Why couldn’t you just take a hint and leave us alone?”

“Did you kill Robert Evans?”

“Don’t ask questions you already know the answer to.”

“She likes to talk. A lot,” Luke said. “Drove me batty getting here. She could talk the whiskers off a cat.”

“Seems to have rubbed off on you.” Norma narrowed her eyes.

“You don’t need to kill me.” Somehow, I didn’t think incessant talking would work with her.

“Your disappearance will be in the newspaper. What better way to tell the idiots of this small town to mind their own business?”

She had a point. I tried to think past the pain. All I could come up with was my full bladder. “I need to use the restroom.”

Norma exhaled heavily. “Luke, take her and guard the door.”

“Can’t Mark do it? She’s given me a headache.”

“Fine. Mark.” She jerked her head toward a door at the end of the room.

“Go.” He yanked me up and gave me a push. “Make it fast.”

These brutes really needed to stop pushing me around. I entered a small, paneled room with no window. A shower, pedestal sink, and toilet. Nothing else. Didn’t matter. I completed my business and pulled my weapons from my pocket. They’d be tricky to use with my left hand, but I was one determined gal.

I checked my phone first and sent Eric a text. *Cabin. Opposite end of fields. Hurry. Will try to get away. They're going to cut off my fingers and toes.* Probably my nose, too, considering their first warning.

Then, convinced Eric and the others were on their way and would rescue me in time, I made sure the pepper-spray nozzle faced away from me, turned on the Taser, and then flung open the door. Mark got the Taser before he knew what happened and fell to the floor in a twitching lump. I then held my breath, aimed the pepper spray at Norma, and squeezed the trigger.

She howled and covered her face, dropping to her knees. I aimed it toward Luke. "Spray or Taser?"

"Neither. Run." He dropped to his knees next to his mother and pretended to cough.

I figured I had a minimum of thirty seconds, maybe longer, depending on how much time it would take to rinse Norma's eyes. I cradled my hurt hand against my chest and darted out of the cabin.

"No more mysteries, no more mysteries" became my chant as I ran, Norma's curses following me. My luck at getting involved in crime solving could only last so long. It might run out today, but I hoped not. Halfway across the field, I veered left toward the river. Even I knew following the path would get me caught.

My phone vibrated. I paused long enough to glance at the screen. A text from Eric. *Stay alive.*

I replied, *Doing my best. Running toward river.*

Pick me up there. I'm hurt. I slipped the phone back in my pocket and resumed my mad dash through a forest I didn't know.

"I'm going to kill you with my bare hands." Mark's voice thundered from somewhere behind me.

Quick. Hide. I dropped behind a thick brush, thankful it hadn't rained in days and waited, my finger on the Taser button. I breathed slow and deep, not wanting anything, no matter how slight, to let him know where I hid.

He stopped in front of my hiding place. I reached out and zapped him, then took off running again when he fell.

Tree branches slapped me in the face and tangled in my hair, yet I kept going. To stop meant death. My breath rasped in my chest. The river halted me. Which way? Down river might lead Mark astray. He'd think I would head upriver toward help, right? I turned left, everything in me longing to go the other way.

I desperately needed to stop and rest. My thumb needed medical attention. I needed Eric and my dog. Tears burned my eyes as my steps faltered, each heavier than the last.

The thwomp-thwomp of a helicopter drew my attention upward. They'd never see me in the trees. I stepped onto the riverbank.

A bullet kicked up dirt at my feet.

I glanced over to see Mark sprinting toward me. I guess my changing direction didn't work. Without a second thought, I jumped into the swift-moving water watching him grow smaller and smaller as the current carried me away. If I didn't drown, I might survive the day. I kept my feet in front of me and fought to keep my head above water. The coldness of the river numbed the pain in my hand.

The helicopter circled overhead again. It was then I realized my phone was in my pocket and now ruined. There was no other way for Eric and Davis to track me unless I could get the attention of the chopper. To do that, I needed to get out of the water and into a clearing, which would make me a sitting goose. The problem would be getting out of the water with a hand that didn't cooperate or provide enough strength to swim across the current.

I bit my lip and swam, kicking as hard as I could toward the opposite bank. Finally I crawled into the bushes to rest.

When my eyes opened, dusk had settled over the trees. No. I didn't want to spend the night alone in the woods. How could I have been foolish enough to fall asleep? I lay there and listened to the sounds of the night. The buzzing of insects and the croaking of frogs relieved me. They'd be silent if someone were around. I proved the fact by sitting up and all sounds around me ceased.

I pushed to my feet and staggered back the way I'd come, staying to the shadows. If Mark still wandered on the other side of the river, I didn't want him to see me. A bullet could reach where a man couldn't.

Wrapping my arms around me to ward off the chill of the night, I tried to focus on what I'd do when I was rescued. I'd want a kiss from Eric first thing, then something to drink, then food. Yeah. Clean, dry clothes would be nice too.

Had they removed the bomb from my car? Had anyone been injured? I hoped not.

I didn't know how long I'd walked before sitting on a termite-eaten log to rest. My stomach had long ago stopped rumbling. My throat felt like sandpaper, and my tongue stuck to the roof of my mouth. Wouldn't it be ironic if my fleeing from the Lakes resulted in me dying of dehydration?

Sighing, I pressed to my feet and continued on, hoping, praying I'd recognize either the exit or entry point. Then, I'd swim back across, hide and wait for Eric to arrive.

Crashing through the brush on the other side of the river halted me. Whispered voices, the flicker of a flashlight. I hunkered down, prepared to wait them out.

"She can't have just disappeared," Norma said. "We didn't find her downriver, so she had to have circled back."

"What if she's on the other side?" Mark asked.

"How would she have done that? Her hand is broken."

"Luke said she's a pretty determined woman."

"So am I. Now find her before the law does."

"Why don't we leave?" Luke asked. "Go to Mexico as planned? Spending all this time looking for a girl who probably drowned is going to get us arrested or killed."

"Look at my face." Norma no longer spoke in hushed tones. "Is it still red from the pepper burn? She assaulted me, she was directly responsible for us destroying millions of dollars' worth of crops, and you want to let her go? We need to make an example of her. We used to be the top dog around here before Evans ratted us out, now this girl. I ought to shoot you right here and let you join your brother in hell."

I put a hand over my mouth to stifle a gasp, holding my breath in anticipation of a gunshot that would end Luke's life. He'd helped me get away. I'd rather he went to jail than get shot by his evil mother.

"Fine. We keep looking," Luke said.

"That's right. We either find her or her body. I'm not stopping until then."

The woman was tenacious, I'd give her that. I smiled knowing I'd caused her pain with my spray. I'd like to do a whole lot more for her, but I had more important things to tend to. Like escape.

I melted back into the shadows and carefully placed each foot, not wanting to snap a twig or send a pebble rolling. Today was easily the longest one of my life.

The exit point. I almost bounded from the trees without looking but froze as the three Lakes stepped into view.

Mark shined a flashlight across the ground. "No fresh prints."

"I told you she probably drowned," Luke said, leaning against a tree. "Mom said it herself. How could she swim with a bum hand?"

I managed, thank you. Two options remained at this point. One, wait until they left, then swim across, or two, keep going until I reached the entry point. Except, they'd be there, too. The best bet was to stay put until they'd moved on, then swim across. I'd figure out my next step then.

When Luke pulled water bottles from the backpack he wore, I almost gave myself up. I'd kill for a drink, I thought and gazed longingly at the river glistening under the moonlight. No, dysentery wasn't something I wanted to experience.

After several minutes of torture watching them guzzle down water, they headed up the path. I closed my eyes in relief. After counting to one hundred, I stepped out and slipped into the water. With this section being where people took their canoes and kayaks from the water, it wasn't nearly as hard to traverse.

I submerged until my eyes and forehead were all that stuck above the surface and scanned the shore. The coast looked clear. I crawled from the water and into the bushes. After several minutes, I headed up the trail, still staying off the main path.

The roar of an engine stopped me in my tracks.

Chapter Twenty-Five

Rescue! Keeping my hand close to my chest, I dashed in the direction of the parking lot. Gunshots had me skidding to a stop. It sounded like World War III ahead of me. All I could do was pray the good guys won.

The shots continued far too long in my opinion. When they finally died down and were replaced with shouting, I crept forward, peering through the branches of a low-hanging tree to the parking lot.

Five squad cars, running police officers, a grim-faced Ann, and three bodies on the ground filled the scene in front of me. I stepped from hiding and froze as several rifles were aimed in my direction.

"Hold your fire." Davis hurried toward me. "Drake, she's here."

One of the men on the other side of the cars turned. Tears streamed down Eric's face as he pushed an officer aside and ran toward me. "You're alive." He gathered me close with his good arm.

I cried out as my hand was caught between us. "It wasn't easy."

He pulled back and cradled my hand in his. "What happened?"

"I punched Luke in the jaw." I glanced over with sadness to see him lying still.

"That's my girl." He leaned his forehead against mine.

"Luke helped me escape, Eric. It's sad that he's dead." I stepped next to the big man's body. He didn't even have a gun on him.

Davis draped a blanket around my shoulders and handed me a water bottle. "He's still a criminal, CJ, but I am glad you had help out there."

I nodded, then guzzled the entire bottle of water. "I want to go home."

"She's free to go," Davis told Eric. "I'll come by later to take her statement."

"Come on, baby." Eric led me to his jeep and settled me into the front seat, clicking the seatbelt into place. "Let's get that hand looked at first."

I couldn't agree more. I leaned my head back and slept until we stopped at the hospital. An hour later, after a cast and a lecture from the doctor about not tucking my thumb in before throwing a punch, I cuddled on my sofa with Caper in my lap and Eric by my side.

Across from us sat Ann, Mags, and Larry. I had no idea where we'd squeeze Davis when he arrived. I'd told everyone I didn't want to tell the harrowing tale twice, so they stared at me while waiting. For the first time since meeting him, I couldn't wait for

Davis to arrive.

"Did you really punch that big man in the face?" Mags's eyes widened. "Did you stand on a rock? Jump? How'd you'd reach?"

I laughed. "I don't know. I just hit him."

"I told you to take self-defense classes," Ann said.

"Yes, you did, and I will. As soon as my thumb heals."

"I'm glad you at least listened to me about the pepper spray and Taser," Mags said. "Now, if you'd had a gun—"

"I'd have been in a gunfight I couldn't have won." I glanced up when Davis entered. *Thank you, God.*

"Uh." He looked around the room. "Mind moving this outside? There's more space."

We trooped outside, either taking a seat at the picnic table or the steps. Davis sat across from me at the table, a pad of paper in front of him. The ever-practical Ann set a lantern I kept in case of power outages next to us.

"I know Luke Waters took you from your home. He drove you to the river where he parked his truck and took you through the woods to the cabin." Davis fixed me with a concerned look. "What I need to know is what happened between then and when we had the confrontation. Are you up to it?"

I nodded. "I'm fine."

"Of course, she is." Mags patted my shoulder. "She's tiny but mighty. I've always known CJ has steel in her bones."

Davis's lips twitched. "She is proving to be quite something."

"My brave girl." Eric gave me a warm look.

"In one of the shows I watch, the victim talked about her life so the abductor would look at her as a person rather than an object. So I talked the entire time about whatever came to mind. Luke probably wanted to shoot himself by the time we reached the cabin." I smiled sadly at the memory of him lying in the parking lot. "I actually thought, fool that I am, that he would have let me go before then. So I punched him."

Drake laughed. "What did he do then?"

"Took me to his mother. She wasn't quite as nice. Luke set me in a chair with plastic on the floor. They were going to cut off parts of me that I'm quite attached to. I had to use the restroom, and Norma actually let me. When I came out, I Tased Mark, sprayed Norma, and ran. Luke told me to, so I did. When I had nowhere else to go, I jumped in the river."

"You're quite the soldier," Larry said, admiration shining from his eyes. "I'm proud to call you my niece."

"Even after I was so mean to you?" I really had thought him a killer at first.

"Yes, even after that." He smiled. "You were only looking out for my sweet Mags. How can I fault you for that?"

I returned my attention to Davis. "What happened at the parking lot?"

"They expected to run into you. Instead, they faced a barricade of law enforcement. Norma fired the first shot. They had no chance of winning the fight."

"Suicide by cop," Ann said. "They knew they'd lost and went out with guns blazing."

"Except for Luke," I pointed out.

She shook her head. "He had a gun. He returned fire. It was under his body when they moved him. He might have been kind to you, but he was still a killer."

I leaned into Eric. "I'm glad it's over and no one else was hurt."

"It's time to get you to bed." Eric stood and ushered me into the house and up the stairs. He tucked me into bed, then sat next to me. "You scared the life out of me."

"Ditto." I caressed his face. "Grams always told me the girl never says these words first, but I don't care. I love you, Eric Drake."

"I love you, Clarice Josephine Turley." He leaned down and gave me a kiss that made me forget all the aches. "I'm glad you're brave enough to be the first this time."

I laughed. "Almost dying convinced me I don't want to waste any more time. I've also decided not to get involved in anymore crime-solving."

Laughter erupted from downstairs. I forgot how un-private a tiny house was.

"Sure you will, sweetheart. Sure you will." Eric joined in with the laughs, then stood. "Sleep well. I'll be right downstairs on the cot. Today took a toll on my shoulder."

"I'm sorry."

"I'll come after you no matter how badly

wounded I am. Always."

I fell sleep to those loving words, and my puppy's warm body curled next to mine.

The End

Stay Tuned for Caper's Dark Adventure, Book 4 in the Tiny House Mysteries. Scan the QR code to learn more.

Did you miss book 1 and 2?

No Small Caper
Caper Goes Missing

Website at www.cynthiahickey.com

Multi-published and Amazon and ECPA Best-Selling author Cynthia Hickey has sold close to a million copies of her works since 2013. She has taught a Continuing Education class at the 2015 American Christian Fiction Writers conference, several small ACFW chapters and RWA chapters, and small writer retreats. She and her husband run the small press, Winged Publications, which includes some of the CBA's best well-known authors. She lives in Arizona and Arkansas, becoming a snowbird, with her husband and one dog. She has nine grandchildren who keep her busy and tell everyone they know that "Nana is a writer".

Connect with me on FaceBook
Twitter
Bookbub
Sign up for my newsletter and receive a free short story
www.cynthiahickey.com

Follow me on Amazon

Enjoy other books by Cynthia Hickey

Fantasy
Fate of the Faes

Shayna
Deema
Kasdeya

Time Travel
The Portal

Tiny House Mysteries
No Small Caper
Caper Goes Missing

Wife for Hire – Private Investigators
Saving Sarah
Lesson for Lacey

A Hollywood Murder
Killer Pose, book 1
Killer Snapshot, book 2
Shoot to Kill, book 3
Kodak Kill Shot, book 4
To Snap a Killer

Shady Acres Mysteries
Beware the Orchids, book 1
Path to Nowhere
Poison Foliage
Poinsettia Madness
Deadly Greenhouse Gases
Vine Entrapment

CLEAN BUT GRITTY

Highland Springs

Murder Live
Say Bye to Mommy
To Breathe Again

Colors of Evil Series

Shades of Crimson
Coral Shadows

The Pretty Must Die Series

Ripped in Red, book 1
Pierced in Pink, book 2
Wounded in White, book 3
Worthy, The Complete Story

Lisa Paxton Mystery Series

Eenie Meenie Miny Mo
Jack Be Nimble
Hickory Dickory Dock

One Hour (A short story thriller)

INSPIRATIONAL
(scroll down to see clean books without inspirational message)

Whisper Sweet Nothings (a short romance)

Nosy Neighbor Series
Anything For A Mystery, Book 1
A Killer Plot, Book 2
Skin Care Can Be Murder, Book 3
Death By Baking, Book 4
Jogging Is Bad For Your Health, Book 5
Poison Bubbles, Book 6
A Good Party Can Kill You, Book 7 (Final)
Nosy Neighbor collection

Christmas with Stormi Nelson

The Summer Meadows Series
Fudge-Laced Felonies, Book 1
Candy-Coated Secrets, Book 2
Chocolate-Covered Crime, Book 3
Maui Macadamia Madness, Book 4
All four novels in one collection

The River Valley Mystery Series
Deadly Neighbors, Book 1
Advance Notice, Book 2
The Librarian's Last Chapter, Book 3
All three novels in one collection

Historical cozy
Hazel's Quest

Historical Romances

Runaway Sue

Taming the Sheriff

Sweet Apple Blossom

A Doctor's Agreement

A Lady Maid's Honor

A Touch of Sugar

Love Over Par

Heart of the Emerald

Finding Love the Harvey Girl Way

Cooking With Love

Guiding With Love

Serving With Love

Warring With Love

All 4 in 1

A Wild Horse Pass Novel

They Call Her Mrs. Sheriff, book 1 (A Western Romance)

Finding Love in Disaster

The Rancher's Dilemma

The Teacher's Rescue

The Soldier's Redemption

Woman of courage Series

A Love For Delicious

Ruth's Redemption

Charity's Gold Rush

Mountain Redemption

Woman of Courage series (all four books)

Short Story Westerns

Desert Rose

Desert Lilly

Desert Belle

Desert Daisy

Flowers of the Desert 4 in 1

Romantic Suspense

Overcoming Evil series

Mistaken Assassin

Captured Innocence

Mountain of Fear

Exposure at Sea

A Secret to Die for

Collision Course

Romantic Suspense of 5 books in 1

The Game

Suspicious Minds

After the Storm

Local Betrayal

Contemporary

Romance in Paradise

Maui Magic

Sunset Kisses

Deep Sea Love

3 in 1

Finding a Way Home
Service of Love
Hillbilly Cinderella
Unraveling Love
I'd Rather Kiss My Horse

Christmas
Dear Jillian
Romancing the Fabulous Cooper Brothers
Handcarved Christmas
The Payback Bride
Curtain Calls and Christmas Wishes
Christmas Gold
A Christmas Stamp
Snowflake Kisses
A Christmas Deception

The Red Hat's Club (Contemporary novellas)

Finally
Suddenly
Surprisingly
The Red Hat's Club 3 – in 1

Short Story

One Hour (A short story thriller)
Whisper Sweet Nothings (a Valentine short romance)

Made in the USA
Columbia, SC
12 September 2023

22787863R00133